||| | ||||| || || | ||||||||||||||| |||

◁ **W9-BSK-881**

Thursday, October 16, 4:05 P.M.

Dear Diary:
I'm practically fainting. Here's the shocking and horrible news: Dad met somebody named Ayanna and kissed her.
At least I didn't see the kiss. I read about it in an e-mail. . . . I'm feeling two things at once. I'm horrified to have found this e-mail, and yet I'm glad that I found it before he did. . . . Reading this secret information both scares me and makes me feel like I could lift a truck with my bare hands. I must act. Without delay.

• •

A *Washington Post* Book of the Week

"Middle-graders looking for a realistic . . . read with laughs and a few misty-eyed moments won't be disappointed." —*Kirkus Reviews*

The Naked Mole-Rat Letters

Mary Amato

Holiday House / New York

Acknowledgments

Thanks to Max and Justine for their comments on the draft.
Thanks also to Paul Sherman, Professor of Animal Behavior at
Cornell University, for information and insights about naked mole-rats.
Any mistakes about the nearly hairless wonders are mine, not his.

Artwork on pages 44, 72, 105, and 229 by Heather Saunders.

Copyright © 2005 by Mary Amato
All Rights Reserved
Printed in the United States of America
www.holidayhouse.com
5   7   9   10   8   6   4

Library of Congress Cataloging-in-Publication Data
Amato, Mary.
The naked mole-rat letters / Mary Amato.— 1st ed.
p. cm.
Summary: When her father begins a long-distance romance with a
Washington, D.C., zookeeper, twelve-year-old Frankie sends fabricated
email letters to the zookeeper in an attempt to end the relationship.
ISBN 0-8234-1927-4 (hardcover)
[1. Honesty—Fiction. 2. Fathers and daughters—Fiction.
3. Email—Fiction. 4. Diaries—Fiction.] I. Title.
PZ7.A49165Nak 2005
[Fic]—dc22   2004052317
ISBN-13: 978-0-8234-1927-2 (hardcover)
ISBN-13: 978-0-8234-2098-8 (paperback)

HOLIDAY HOUSE is registered in the U.S. Patent and Trademark Office.

In memory of
my mom and Eunice

To: **Robert Wallop <wallop@dman.com>**
From: **Ayanna Bayo <ratlady@wz.org>**
Received: **Thursday, Oct. 16, 10:00 A.M.**
Subject: **Kiss**

Dear Robert:
Just a line to say thank you for the wonderful dinner last night. I enjoyed the food, the conversation, and—especially—the kiss. Will our paths cross again?
Hopefully yours,
Ayanna
P.S. You left a small bag of conference brochures by the feeding station. I'll mail it to you.

Thursday, October 16, 4:05 P.M.

Dear Diary:
I'm practically fainting. Here's the shocking and horrible news: Dad met somebody named Ayanna and kissed her.
At least I didn't see the kiss. I read about it in an e-mail and called Beth right away.

1

"Oh Frankie, maybe your dad will fall in love with her and ask her to marry him," she said, as if that would be a good thing.

"Beth!" I yelled into the phone. "This is my life we're talking about here. Not some stupid, romantic TV show. I don't want a step-mother."

"Why not?"

"Why not? Are you crazy? Do you have any idea what it would mean for some stranger to walk in and take over your whole life?" I listened to the silence on the other end of the line and realized that Beth didn't have a clue.

"But Frankie, if you got to know her, then she wouldn't be a stranger and—"

"Forget it, Beth," I said, and hung up. I've never hung up on Beth before, which just goes to show you how upset all this is making me.

I don't know who Ayanna is or why any-body would have the e-mail name "ratlady." Dad must have met her on the sorted (sordid?) streets of Washington, D.C. (He went there three days ago for that music conference and is getting back any minute.) I'm sure it's all a big mistake. This woman just needs to know that their paths will never cross again.

I'm feeling two things at once. I'm horrified to have found this e-mail, and yet I'm glad that I found it before he did. How can a person be horrified and glad at the same time? It's like drinking something that's as foul as poison and as fizzy as soda. Well, I'm horrified that Dad would have this little romantic fling, and I'm glad because I can do something to stop it from going any further. Now I know what Ms. Young meant when she said information is power. Reading this secret information both scares me and makes me feel like I could lift a truck with my bare hands. I must act. Without delay.

To: Ayanna Bayo <ratlady@wz.org>
From: Robert Wallop <wallop@dman.com>
Sent: Thursday, Oct. 16, 4:16 P.M.
Subject: Re: Kiss

Ratlady:
    I don't know who you are. But this is just a note to say please don't bother e-mailing again.

My father, Robert Wallop, is extremely busy taking care of us children. Perhaps he did not mention the little fact that he has children. He does. Three. There's me. I'm in seventh grade, and I don't require any care, actually. But I have two younger brothers who require constant care on account of their severe, deliberating illnesses. Skip is nine, and Nutter is five. Our real names are Francine, Samuel, and George, but everybody calls us by our nicknames.

Also you should know that my father has several diseases, so kissing him is not a good idea.

Sincerely,
Frankie Wallop

To: **Robert Wallop <wallop@dman.com>**
From: **Ayanna Bayo <ratlady@wz.org>**
Received: **Thursday, Oct. 16, 4:45 P.M.**
Subject: **Re: Kiss**

Dear Frankie:

My name is Ayanna Bayo. Please call me Ayanna. Your father and I met here in Washington, D.C. He did talk about you and your brothers, although he failed to mention the debilitating condition of your brothers. I'm sure you're a big help to the whole family. Has your father arrived home yet?

Curiously,

Ayanna

To: **Ayanna Bayo <ratlady@wz.org>**
From: **Robert Wallop <wallop@dman.com>**
Sent: **Thursday, Oct. 16, 4:50 P.M.**
Subject: **My Dad**

Ms. Ratlady:

My father probably didn't mention the condition of my brothers because he is ashamed of them. On account of their many problems, they have very ugly faces, and yet we have to look at them all the time because they require constant care. They drool and have diarrhea every minute of every day. You should be happy you live so far away.

Sincerely,

Frankie Wallop

P.S. My father arrived home, read your e-mail, and

mentioned that he simply didn't have time to reply.
Ever. So this is good-bye.

Still Thursday, 10:00 P.M.

Dear Diary:

My cup fizzeth over with joy. I took care of the situation with "speed and a plum," as Ms. Young used to say. (A plumb? Aplomb?) I erased all the evidence. I'm surprisingly good at all this for someone who is normally so honest. No need to worry anymore about Ratlady.

Dad came home from the airport at five o'clock. I didn't have time to look at him too closely because he had to take Mrs. Whitehead home. Even though I'm twelve, he doesn't trust me to baby-sit Skip and Nutter for overnights. Mrs. Whitehead is the new minister's wife, and she's about as fun as burned toast. Anyway, when Dad came home and took off his coat, I noticed something suspicious. Usually he looks exactly the same every day of his life. He either wears baggy khaki pants with a Heartstrings T-shirt (which is black) or a Red Beet Ramblers T-shirt (which is maroon). That's it. He's big. But he's not fat. With his curly hair and his bushy beard—reddish, like my hair—he looks like a bear wearing hand-me-downs. Today his beard was trimmed. He was wearing blue jeans and a very hip, new, tie-dyed shirt that said, BE WILD AT THE NATIONAL ZOO.

"Hey, you look cool, Dad," Nutter said.

"I am cool," Dad said, and scooped him up in a hug.

It is highly unusual for Dad to actually look cool.

Next we had a very normal dinner. Frozen ravioli. Here's how it went. . . .

Skip kicked Nutter under the table. Nutter kicked Skip.

"Would you guys knock it off?" Dad asked in his usual highly effective way.

"He started it!" Skip yelled.

"I did not!" Nutter cried.

The menacing cloud that is Skip's personality settled over his face; and when Dad went into the kitchen for napkins, Skip gave one last kick.

But Nutter, the human squirrel, is way too fast for Skip. Nutter scooted off his chair, which meant that Skip ended up kicking the table's leg instead of Nutter's.

This caused a brief tabletop earthquake, and Nutter's milk tipped over into my lap. Nutter, of course, laughed. The cloud lifted off Skip's face, and he laughed so hard he fell off his chair. Then Dad came in, and he grinned at Skip and Nutter like they were stand-up comedians. "I guess I don't need to visit a zoo," Dad said. "I live in one."

Nutter hopped back up on his chair, scratched under his arms, and said, "Ooo, ooo, ooo," in his loudest monkey voice.

They all cracked up, and I sat there, dripping with milk, unable to believe my ears. If I had kicked the table leg and spilled the milk, Dad would have had a screaming fit and grounded me for three months. That's the injustice of my life.

"Speaking of zoos," Dad said, "the National Zoo was right down the block from my hotel, so I got you each a souvenir."

Miracle of miracles. Dad picked out very cool stuff. A stage paint kit for me—a set of special face paints (*not* babyish) with a guide for creating characters and special effects. Night-vision binoculars for Skip (to go with his spy recorder and digital spy camera). And the cutest little furry backpack in the shape of a koala for Nutter. Right away Nutter put it on and started running around the house making jungle noises. I swear he looks like a little koala carrying around a baby koala on his back. When he is not being annoying, he is beyond cute.

Well it's bedtime now. When Dad is asleep, I'm going to sneak down to the dining room (that's where we keep the computer) and make sure Ms. Ratlady has indeed ceased her rootless (frootless? fruitless?) communication. Luckily Dad is not an e-mail person.

Dear Ayanna:

I'm afraid that it's too late for me to call, so I thought I'd send a quick note.

I'm happy that my conference was scheduled in the hotel near the zoo.

And I'm glad that I decided to pop over to the zoo on Monday to pick up souvenirs for my kids.

And I'm delighted that it rained, which sent me running into the small mammal house for cover, so that I could literally knock you off your feet. (Sorry about that!)

And I'm thrilled that you agreed to meet me for dinner that first night.

And I'm overjoyed that we were able to spend so much time together during the rest of my stay. (I'm sure I didn't miss much by ditching the meetings on Wednesday. Hope you didn't get into trouble for calling in sick!) I can't tell you how much fun it was.

Yours truly,
Robert
P.S. Thanks for helping to pick out the gifts for my kids. They loved them. At bedtime Nutter wouldn't take his backpack off, so believe it or not, he's sleeping with a koala on his back.

Still Thursday, 11:00 P.M.

Dear Diary:

I can't believe it. While I was writing in here, Dad was sending Ratlady an e-mail! I found it in the sent box. And it's disgusting. They spent time together, whatever that means. He didn't even go to his meetings. He doesn't sound like himself at all. He sounds like someone who swallowed a soap opera.

I thought my heart was going to stop beating when I read it, so I came back to my room to lie down. Obviously drastic measures are required. Should I act now or wait for her next move?

What I really should do is go to bed. I need my sleep. Tomorrow after school is the audition for the school play. The play is *The Miracle Worker*, and I am dying to play the part of Annie Sullivan. She is the miracle worker of the play because she saves Helen Keller (who can't see, can't hear, and hasn't yet learned to speak) from the depths of darkness and despair by teaching her sign language. She did this by pressing the signs for letters into Helen's hand. She taught Helen to *feel* words. It's a true story. Annie is the most dramatic role in the history of theater, and I just know I'm going to get the part. With my long, red hair and my mature nose, I look exactly like an Annie Sullivan. Well if I don't get Annie, then I'll definitely get Helen, which is the other leading role. I like Annie better because she has the most lines. Helen doesn't really have any because she doesn't know how to talk.

But if I don't do something about Ratlady now, then I'll probably toss and turn in a fretful state of worry all night.

I'm going to act now. As Ms. Young always said, "She who hesitates is lost."

To: **Ayanna Bayo <ratlady@wz.org>**
From: **Robert Wallop <wallop@dman.com>**
Sent: **Thursday, Oct. 16, 11:16 P.M.**
Subject: **Big Mistake**

Dear Ratlady:

When my father sent his e-mail, he forgot to mention that he is taking special drugs for allergies that make people say ridiculous things. He is allergic to many things, which makes him annoying to live with because his nose is always full of snot.

Sincerely,

Frankie Wallop

P.S. My brothers and I did not like the gifts from the zoo that you helped pick out. They were silly, or shall I say lucrative? You must not know children at all. Please do not e-mail my father anymore.

To: Robert Wallop <wallop@dman.com>
From: Ayanna Bayo <ratlady@wz.org>
Received: Thursday, Oct. 16, 11:43 P.M.
Subject: Re: Big Mistake

Dear Frankie:

My, you're up late. It's almost midnight in Indiana. The east is one hour ahead of you, so I'm up even later.

I'm sorry that you thought your gifts were ludicrous, but you have to admit it was nice of your father to think of you. You may be right. I might not know children well; I have none of my own. But my friends say that I act like a child! (I take it as a compliment.)

I do know small mammals—particularly naked mole-rats—very well. I am the naked mole-rat keeper at the National Zoo, hence my e-mail nickname: "ratlady."

Naked mole-rats are wrinkly, nearly hairless creatures that burrow in tunnels underground. Most people think they're ugly. I'm quite fond of them. Sometimes even ugly creatures prove to be worth loving once you get to know them. Perhaps you feel that way about your brothers?

Sleepily yours,

Ayanna

To: **Ayanna Bayo <ratlady@wz.org>**
From: **Robert Wallop <wallop@dman.com>**
Sent: **Thursday, Oct. 16, 11:50 P.M.**
Subject: **Re: Big Mistake**

Dear Ratlady:

Indeed I should be in bed, for I have a big audition tomorrow. But the seriousness of this whole episode has caused me much anxiety.

I just want you to know that I am the e-mailer in the family, and I will be checking ALL the messages. My dad won't let me get my own address yet. "One address is fine for the whole family," he says. He hates e-mailing for many reasons and only writes to be polite.

Also, you should know that he is allergic to small mammals. He probably didn't mention this because he was trying to be polite. My brothers,

15

by the way, are not only ugly, but also they're very cruel to others. There is nothing you can do to change them. They're genetically mogrified to be cruel. They especially do not like adult females.

Sincerely,

Frankie Wallop

P.S. This is it. So good-bye for good.

Friday, October 17, 2:15 P.M.

Dear Diary:

I should be running laps around the field right now, but I told my P.E. teacher that I am suffering from agonizing stomach cramps due to the leftover tuna salad I had for lunch. This is a lie. I was afraid that if I told her the truth, she wouldn't believe me. The truth is that I'm suffering from severe stress, and I've had a total of five heart attacks today.

I must have done an excellent job of acting the part of a girl racked with stomach cramps because she sent me to the nurse's office, where I am now.

I confess that I expected more from a junior high nurse's office. This is a room with a cot. There isn't even a nurse in here! Mrs. Willa, the secretary, looked me over and said, "You might as well lie down and do your homework, if you got any. Kill two birds with one stone."

I do have homework, but I'd rather use my time to chronical (chronicul? chronicle?) the horrible and fateful day that I've had thus far. In case you have forgotten, dear Diary, I have the audition of a lifetime in exactly sixty minutes, and my nerves are like sticks of dynamite. If I write about what has happened, then perhaps I can clear my brain before I explode. I will start at the beginning so that I don't leave anything out.

Early this morning, I was fast asleep in the dark, cozy nest of my bed when I heard a familiar, nuttery voice yell, "CANNON-BALL!"

Before the word had a chance to sink deeply into my brain, a flying object otherwise known as Nutter landed on me.

Heart attack number one.

"Ouch!" I yelled.

Nutter screamed and jumped off me like I was a mummy rising from a grave. "I thought you were in the bathroom!" he said. "I thought the bed was empty and the covers were just bumpy. And what are those pink worms in your hair?"

"They're not worms." I got out of bed. "They're hair curlers."

"Don't ever scare me like that again." He held out his little hands to show me they were shaking.

"Well, why were you jumping on my bed anyway?"

"I like to."

"Jump on your own bed."

"Your bed's better. Your blanket is 'swimming pool blue.' And what are those curler things for anyway?"

"You roll your hair up in them and sleep on them, and in the morning you have curly hair. Mrs. Whitehead let me borrow them."

I looked at the clock and had the second heart attack of the day. 7:30! How could it be

7:30? My alarm clock was set for 6:45. Did I turn it off and go back to sleep?

I had wanted to wake up early so that I would have plenty of time to check the e-mail situation and to fix my hair and get especially dressed up for the audition. Now I would barely have time to get out the door.

Skip walked in. "Dad said I'm supposed to wake you up. Your head looks weird."

"Thanks a lot! Why didn't he think of that an hour ago?"

Nutter grinned at Skip. "I woked her up when I landed on her butt."

I shoved Skip and Nutter out the door.

Nutter glued his hands and feet to my doorway. "Skip and me want to practice diving on your bed."

"Go dive on your head!" I peeled him off and slammed the door.

The third heart attack came when I tried to take the curlers out of my hair. Mrs. Whitehead showed me how to do it, but I must have done it wrong. My hair was all twisted and tangled, and I couldn't get the curlers out.

I was not prepared for what I'd find in the

kitchen. Dad should have been making Skip's and Nutter's lunches and listening to serious news on the radio. Instead he had the rock-and-roll station on and was singing. Skip and Nutter were sliding around in their stocking feet, playing air guitars.

"Come on, Frankie, join in." Dad handed me a box of foil like it was a microphone. Then he squinted at my hair. "Are those curlers in there?"

"Yes! And I can't get them out."

The three of them started laughing.

I glared at Dad. "This is not funny. You have to get them out."

Dad tore out half my hair getting the curlers out, and when I looked in the mirror . . . well, that was the fourth heart attack. My hair looked exactly like a nest made by a blind squirrel on drugs.

I had no choice but to stick my head under the faucet.

At school I couldn't concentrate. In first period math I had to solve a problem on the board; and while I was doing it, everybody was laughing. At first I thought it was because

I was doing the math problem wrong. Then I heard Jerry Parks whisper to Johnny Nye, "What are those?" I felt the back of my head, and my heart absolutely stopped. Two curlers sticking out like Frankenstein bolts.

I tried to pull them out. No such luck. So I calmly put the chalk down and walked over to Mr. Peter's desk. "May I please go to the bathroom?"

Last year, Ms. Young would have let me go right away. Ms. Young was the most wonderful sixth-grade teacher in the world. She should have asked to teach seventh grade so that I could have her again this year.

I should have known that Mr. Peter wouldn't let me go to the bathroom. Mr. Peter is not a living, breathing human being with a heart that has attacks. Mr. Peter is a battery-operated calculator in the shape of a human being. And his batteries aren't showing any signs of wearing out. "You can go after the lesson," he said, and wrote me a pass.

For the remainder of the lesson, everyone stared at me while I sat at my desk and fumigated (fumed? emitted fumes?). Beth tried to

21

catch my eye, but for her own good I wouldn't look up. If I had looked at her, my angry gaze would have burned her eyeballs out. How could my best friend, who sits right next to me, have missed two curlers sticking out the back of my head? *Are you blind, Beth?*

For that matter, how could Dad have missed them? Maybe if he hadn't been dancing around and singing to the radio he would have done a better job. And why was he in such a good mood this morning anyway?

With horror I realized that he was acting like someone in love. Was he in a good mood because he assumed Ratlady was going to e-mail him back?

Would Ratlady ignore my message and e-mail him anyway? Maybe she already did and he read it before I woke up. Maybe that's why he was in such a good mood.

The bell rang and Mr. Peters stopped droning and dismissed class. Now I wasn't going to have enough time to get the curlers out and get to my next class on time.

There was only one thing to do: ditch. I'd never committed a school-related crime before.

I had to do it—for my hair and my family. I went to my locker, put on my coat, and started walking to the front door. I realized that my heart must have started up again because it was beating like crazy. No teachers in sight. Five more steps and I'd be at the door. Five, four, three, two—

The Troll stepped in front of the door. Her name is Ms. Trolly, and she's the new guidance counselor. She pronounces her name like "troll" with a "y," and she looks like one, too, which is why everybody calls her The Troll.

"Pass?" she asked.

"Yes, I'd like to pass, thank you."

"That is not what I meant. I'm on hall duty. I need to see your pass."

"Pass?"

"A note from the office that says you have permission to leave the building," she explained.

"Oh, a *pass*," I said, and started fumbling around in my pockets as if I had one. "I just had it. . . ."

"Your name is?"

"Frankie Wallop."

"Wallop!" The Troll exclaimed. "I've heard about you." From the way her face cracked into a smile, I knew that she had heard good things about me. Could I use my straight-A reputation to ditch school? What kind of person would that make me?

"Your father owns Heartstrings, that music shop, doesn't he?" She pressed her clipboard against her chest.

"Yes. He directs the Presbyterian Church choir, too," I added. "And I sing in it, of course. Every Sunday." I smiled angelically. "I'm supposed to go to the dentist, and I'm really late." From the depths of my pocket, my fingers grabbed a piece of paper, the bathroom pass from Mr. Peter. I pulled it out and waved it with straight-A confidence.

"Fine," she said, and opened the door.

Before she could look at the paper more closely, I stuffed it into my pocket and hustled out. What an amazing discovery. Somebody like Johnny Nye would need a letter signed by God to get out of school in the middle of the day, whereas I could probably waltz out by flashing a gum wrapper.

Still I wasn't home free. I had to get home without being seen by anyone who would tell Dad. I tried to make myself invisible as I walked past the gas station and the post office by looking straight ahead and taking smooth, steady steps. My town, Pepper Blossom, seems like a particularly small and very highly populated town when you're ditching school. I took the side road, avoiding Main Street where Dad would be working in the shop, and cut through the church lot. The minister's car was the only thing there. I walked quickly, feeling as naked as that emperor who had no clothes. It felt like every window had a face in it, staring at me as I walked by. This must be how criminals like Johnny Nye feel all the time. I couldn't believe I was actually doing it.

The hardest part would be getting past our next-door neighbor's house. Mrs. Holmes sees all and tells all. When I got to our street, I realized why I felt so naked. I had left my backpack at school. With my house key. There was only one way to get in: Ask Mrs. Holmes for our spare key.

As I walked up the path to her house, I reminded myself that the Frankie Wallop she knows would never lie, which meant that I could lie and she would believe me.

Knock. Knock.

The door opened and there she was, short and round and cheery as a pumpkin. "Hi, Sweetheart. Something wrong?"

I smiled innocently. "Nothing's wrong. I just forgot my key."

"But why aren't you in school, Sweet-heart?"

"Well, Ms. Trolly let me come home because . . ."

Why? Why? While I was thinking of a reason, something Ms. Young used to say kept running through my mind: Oh, what a tangled web we weave when first we practice to deceive. It's true. Once you get caught up in lying, it's hard to pull yourself out. "Ms. Trolly let me come home because I forgot my notebook," I finally said, "and although they usually don't let kids come home in the middle of the day, she let me because . . . it's my birthday." Well that last part was stupid. But it was too late to take it back.

"Glory be!" Mrs. Holmes clapped her chubby hands together. "Your birthday!"

It worked. When I got home, the first thing I did was untangle the curlers from my hair and stick my head under the faucet again. Then I checked e-mail. Last night, I had sent a series of highly effective e-mails to Ratlady and deleted all the evidence. Did my lies convince her to back off, or did she sneak a reply to my father's ludicrous letter?

Nothing. No mail from Ratlady. And no more letters from Dad to her. Hurray. Hurrah. Hurroo.

Dad will assume that she doesn't want to return his e-mail. His feelings might be hurt, but he'll get over it and forget her soon enough. Now things can get back to normal. *I* can get back to normal. I'm not the type of person to lie and ditch school. I'm the type of person to succeed in everything I do, which is why it's dangerous for me to start breaking laws. I could become a highly successful criminal if I wanted to. But I don't want to be a criminal. I want to be a miracle worker like Annie Sullivan. I want to be famous for doing good things for those less fortunate than myself.

Whew! I have to stop writing now. The bell is about to ring. The good news is that I'm feeling better. Writing helps. Thank you, dear Diary.

Now I must get psyched up for the audition. On my way to the drama room, I shall pretend to be a teacher walking to my first day on the job. I will be nervous, yet confident. Spunky, yet mature. Very Annie Sullivan. Wish me luck.

Still Friday, 9:00 P.M.

At last a chance to write!

The audition was terrifying—all the eighth-graders looked down their noses at us seventh-graders. It wasn't anything like Ms. Young's auditions back in elementary school. Mr. Haxer is the director. His first name is Justin, and he looks like a movie star. Beth and I agreed to always refer to him as Justin Haxer when we talk about him. He wears this black leather jacket all the time, and I noticed that he smiled more at me than anybody else, which probably made Beth jealous. Beth has a problem with jealousy. At the end of the audition he told us not to get our hopes up and reminded us that it was unusual for seventh-graders to get a lead or to even make the play; however a "star can rise up from any grade." He looked right at me when he said that. I think he was preparing the eighth-graders for the fact that he is going to give the part of Annie Sullivan to me, a seventh-grader. He's going to post the cast list on Monday after school. Today is Friday. I'm going to fall into a comma (coma?) over the weekend.

I wanted to sit down right away and write about the audition, but I didn't have time. I had to hurry over to Mrs. Whitehead's house to pick up Nutter. Beth tagged along. Nutter is supposed to go to Mrs. Whitehead's whenever I have something after school—such as a highly important audition. The poor kid hates it. I don't blame him. Skip is now old enough to walk home and stay home by himself. So he was already here when we arrived. He jumped on me before I could get through the door.

"Listen. . . ." He dragged me over to the answering machine and pushed the button.

"Mr. Wallop, this is Ms. Trolly, the new counselor at the junior high school. I'm calling to let you know your daughter, Francine, missed second period today. She said that she had a dentist's appointment. However the main office has no record of permission. I'm sure this is a mistake on our part, but please call me on Monday to confirm. My number is . . ."

"You're in big trouble." Skip was drooling, he was so excited. Skip's main idea of fun is seeing other people get into trouble.

Beth was so shocked that she couldn't even talk.

"I had to get the curlers out of my hair," I whispered to her. "And check e-mail, if you know what I mean."

Nutter didn't get it. He just looked at me and asked, "Do you have cavities?"

"Yes," I said to Nutter. "Seventeen cavities. But I went to the dentist. And I'm not going to get into trouble." I glared at Skip.

"How are you going to get out of this?" he asked.

How indeed? I pressed the DELETE button on the machine.

Beep. No more trouble.

"What if I tell?" Skip asked.

"You won't."

"How do you know?"

"Because I'll give you a dollar if you don't. And if you do, I'll take it back." The one thing Skip likes more than seeing people get into trouble is making money.

I gave him a dollar.

"My lips are sealed," Skip said. "But the school will just keep calling."

I got out a piece of paper, surprised at how natural all these criminal activities felt to me.

October 17

Dear Ms. Trolly:

Thank you for the phone call. Sorry, I forgot to send a note in with Frankie. Please excuse her. She had to go to the dentist.

Sincerely,

Robert Wallop

"Frankie, what are you doing?" Beth looked at me like I was robbing a bank. "You can't do this!"

"I'll turn it in on Monday, and everything will be fine."

"What does the note say?" Nutter asked.

The front door opened. "Hey, kids!" Dad called out.

I handed Nutter a dollar and whispered, "It says, Don't say anything about this to Dad."

Nutter grinned. Then he turned around and ran into Dad's arms. "Look what Frankie just gave me!"

Dad picked him up. "A whole dollar. How come?"

"Because she's got seventeen cavities." He

clapped his hand over his mouth. "But she doesn't want you to know."

Beth looked at me, panicking. She is definitely not a good person to have around at times like this. If Dad took one look at her face, he'd know everything.

Luckily Dad wasn't paying attention to Beth. He was busy having a little guilt trip of his own. "Oh, when was the last time I brought you guys to the dentist?" He set Nutter down. "Frankie, if you have a cavity, we'd better get you an appointment."

"She already went to the dentist," Nutter said.

I laughed. "Ha-ha. Just kidding, Dad. I don't have any cavities."

"Let me see. Open up."

He came toward me. I was trying to figure out a way to stuff the note into my pocket without seeming too obvious when the doorbell rang.

Dad opened the door.

"Surprise!" In walked Next-Door Nosy, Mrs. Holmes, with a fluffy, white angel food cake dripping with gooey pink frosting and dotted with sugary gumdrops.

We were all speechless.

"Now I'm sure you already got a cake, Robert. But I couldn't resist." She handed me the cake.

I turned as pink as the frosting. I should have said thank you, but I was too busy thinking, *Please don't tell him that I lied to you about my birthday when I should have been in class!*

"Well, that looks delicious, Evelyn," Dad said. "What a special treat. We didn't have anything planned for dessert tonight. Thank you!"

"Nothing planned for dessert?" She looked at us a little sadly and headed out the door. "Well I couldn't let the day go by—" Stopping halfway out, she turned and delivered her usual by-the-way question: "By the way, Robert, anyone special on the horizon?"

That's one thing about Mrs. Holmes that I can't stand. She asks Dad this every time she sees him, as if he doesn't already have us. Dad, by the way, always has the same, joking response: "There's so many, I can't keep up with them!"

But this time he paused and rubbed his beard and said, "One of these days, Evelyn, I'll surprise you and say yes."

Mrs. Holmes thought this was hilarious and laughed all the way home.

I was trying to decide what he meant by this, but I couldn't concentrate. Nutter was jumping up and down. "Cake! Cake!"

"*After* dinner," Dad said.

Beth left, and we sat down to dinner.

Although I felt a little guilty that Mrs. Holmes went to all that trouble when it wasn't my birthday, it didn't stop me from having a fat piece. Deeceeelicious.

After dinner I checked e-mail again. No sign of Ratlady.

The need to lie is coming to a close. The e-mails took care of Ratlady. The note will take care of The Troll. No harm done in letting Mrs. Holmes think it's my birthday. All's well that ends well.

Methinks I shall go now to bed and dream of working with Justin Haxer . . . good night!

You will not believe what just happened.

I was half asleep and half practicing my Annie Sullivan lines when I noticed a soft hum coming from downstairs. It was Dad talking on the phone, which was odd. Dad's not a talker. Could it possibly be The Troll calling this late at night? I wondered. Could my little plan to send in the forged note be ruined before Monday rolled around?

Quietly I crept into the upstairs hallway and picked up the other phone.

"I thought you'd enjoy eating with your hands," a woman was saying, and I had my final heart attack of the day. The caller was Ratlady! I could tell right away because her voice had a little accent; she didn't sound like anybody I'd ever met before. The Rat had phoned because she knew I'd delete her e-mails!

It's very hard to have a heart attack and remain perfectly quiet, but I struggled to control my breathing so that they wouldn't hear me on the line. "Next time," she continued, "give me a little warning, and I'll cook you a homemade vegetable curry."

Dad laughed, but his voice was hushed. He didn't want us to hear. "Sounds exotic. We don't even have Chinese food here. We have two restaurants. There's the Hilltop when you want to go fancy. That's where the tourists go. And there's Mae's for everything else. Mae makes mashed potatoes that stick with you for a week."

The woman laughed. "I'd like to try those."

"You should! Maple County isn't exciting, but it has its own quiet charm. Like I said, people from all over Indiana come to Pepper Blossom this time of year just to see the trees and to come to the festival I told you about. Right now it's like the hills are on fire, there's so much color."

"Maybe I'll surprise you and show up."

Dad laughed. "*That* would really get the peppervine going!"

"What?"

"The gossip channel. Usually it's called the grapevine. Gossip is so big in Pepper Blossom, we call it the peppervine. If you sneeze in Pepper Blossom in the morning, by noon everybody will hear that you've got a cold."

She laughed. "Next time you come to Washington, I'll have to take you to the Shenandoahs—you'd love Skyline Drive."

They were talking about seeing each other again! I wondered what they had talked about before I picked up the phone. I bet she ratted on me and told him about me reading his e-mail and e-mailing her back. Now I'm going to be in big trouble.

I held my breath and listened to the rest of the conversation. Dad tried to convince her to take up the mountain dulcimer, saying how easy it is to learn. He says the same thing to everybody, but the way he said it to her was different. And the way she laughed at everything he said made my stomach burn. As they said good-bye to each other, I put down the phone very gently, even though what I really wanted to do was slam it and scream.

When I got back into bed, I couldn't sleep. Their voices kept talking to each other in my mind. Dad had sounded like he was crawling to her through the telephone line.

So I got up to write.

It's not fair. She's all the way in Washington, D.C., and Dad's here in Indiana, and all those miles should keep them apart. How can he fall in love with a rat who calls when she was told not to bother us anymore?

Why isn't Mom here? Why can't it be the way it's supposed to be? Now I don't know what to do. I feel like I can't even talk to Beth about it. She wouldn't understand. I guess I have to figure it out for myself.

To: **Ayanna Bayo <ratlady@wz.org>**
From: **Robert Wallop <wallop@dman.com>**
Sent: **Saturday, Oct. 18, 7:05 A.M.**
Subject: **Phone Call**

Dear Ratlady:

Don't ever call again. When my dad wakes up, I know I'm going to get into trouble for reading his e-mails. He'll probably take away all my computer

privileges forever and lock me in my room. Do you *like* being a troublemaker?
—Frankie Wallop

To: Ayanna Bayo <ratlady@wz.org>
From: Robert Wallop <wallop@dman.com>
Sent: Saturday, Oct. 18, 9:05 A.M.
Subject: Secret

Ms. Bayo:
When my father woke up, he didn't mention anything about the e-mails. If you kept it a secret, then please ignore the e-mail I sent you earlier. Except I don't want you to ignore the first sentence. Please don't call again.
Thank you,
Frankie Wallop

To: Robert Wallop <wallop@dman.com>
From: Ayanna Bayo <ratlady@wz.org>
Received: Saturday, Oct. 18, 11:58 A.M.
Subject: Re: Secret

Dear Frankie:

I honestly don't want to cause trouble. I believe that correspondence between two people should be private. That's why I didn't tell your father that you e-mailed me. I wouldn't read a letter addressed to someone else, and I wouldn't allow any other person to read a letter addressed to me. I would hope that you would do the same.

I really enjoyed meeting your dad. Human beings are social animals. Grown-ups enjoy making friends just as kids do.

Truthfully yours,

Ayanna

P.S. Do you have one best friend or lots of good friends?

P.P.S. I hope the big audition went well. I admire you for even trying. I am a very shy person and terrified of being onstage. When I was your age, I enjoyed working backstage on a number of plays. One of the things I love about my job is that I get to work "backstage" at the zoo. The naked mole-rats are the stars. I guess I am the stage manager. I take care of all the props and scenery.

Ms. Bayo:

I know what you're trying to do. You're trying to get all chummy with me. Well, it's not going to work.

As for your job, it sounds like a nightmare for the nose. I've been to the small mammal house at the Indianapolis Zoo, and it smelled horrible. My guess is that anyone who works there smells horrible, too.

I, for one, wouldn't want to be stuck inside all day with rodents for company. What can you possibly get out of watching a bunch of dirty rats who aren't even smart enough to grow fur?

—F. W.

P.S. Beth Jamison used to be my best friend (and she still wants to be), but I'm having doubts. There is a lot about life that she doesn't understand. I have lots of other friends, but they aren't good ones. They get jealous of my talents. I've gotten the lead role in every play I've ever tried out for. Some people are just born "star material," and some people are born stagehands. I know that once the play starts, I'll find a new best friend—probably whoever gets the role of Helen Keller, since I'll be Annie Sullivan.

To: Robert Wallop <wallop@dman.com>
From: Ayanna Bayo <ratlady@wz.org>
Received: Saturday, Oct. 18, 12:20 P.M.
Subject: Re: Dirty Rats

Dear Frankie:

The small mammal house does have its own particular smell. It smells like home to me. Is that disgusting? I do take a shower and wear a clean uniform every day, in case you were wondering.

As for naked mole-rats, they are actually smart and clean in their own way.

It is smart for them NOT to have fur. They live in underground burrows in deserts (in East Africa). Their underground home stays warm all year round, so they don't need fur. In fact their thin, bare skin helps them to change their body temperature to suit the temperature changes in their environment. In this way they're similar to reptiles—who are also thin-skinned—like chameleons.

They are remarkably clean, too. Did you know that they have what we call a "toilet chamber"? This means that they have created a special room just for peeing and pooping. That way diseases don't get spread around. Isn't that smart?

Attached is a sketch of the tunnel system I have created for the naked-mole rats here at the zoo so you can picture it. (I like to draw.)

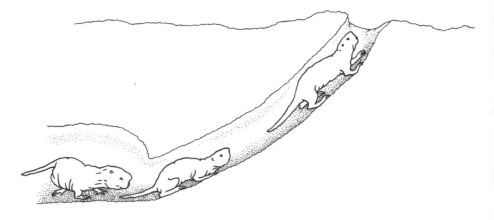

I should mention that from time to time they do roll around in their own pee and poop. That may not seem so smart, but they have a good reason for it. They identify colony mates by smell, so rolling around in their own poop is a way of labeling their colony membership.

Naked mole-rats, like a lot of animals, are very territorial. That means if an intruder digs into their burrow, the naked mole-rats will attack.

One of the things I've learned is that you can't really judge an animal by its appearance or actions before getting to know it. Most often, there's a good reason why an animal acts the way it does.

Zoologically yours,

Ayanna

P.S. It's funny that you should talk about how some people are "star material" and some people are stagehands. In naked mole-rat colonies, each mole-rat has a job. There are breeders, soldiers, housekeepers, and even a queen! One of the things that biologists are trying to discover is why mole-rats take on these jobs. What does it take to become queen, for example? Can you tell I'm fascinated by all this?

To: **Ayanna Bayo <ratlady@wz.org>**
From: **Robert Wallop <wallop@dman.com>**
Sent: **Saturday, Oct. 18, 12:31 P.M.**
Subject: **No Phone Calls**

Ms. Bayo:

Your naked mole-rats sound disgusting. If you like them, then I guess you've chosen the right profession. Just don't expect everybody else to like them.

I don't have time to send any more e-mails today. I am sending you this last one because I forgot to tell you something. Our house is very small. We live in a trailer, actually, and sleep on little bunks next to each other. It's all we can afford because Dad hasn't been selling very many instruments. So if anybody is talking on the phone late at night, it wakes everybody else up. My poor brothers really need their sleep on account of their illnesses. The doctor said that if their sleep is interrupted, their health will rapidly detonate.

You should also know that this time of year is the busiest time of all for my dad's shop. If you bother him there, he might not be able to sell any of his dulcimers and then we won't be able to afford all the doctor's bills.

Seriously yours,

Frankie

P.S. Since you believe that correspondence between two people should be private, does this mean that you promise not to tell my dad that I am e-mailing you?

To: **Robert Wallop <wallop@dman.com>**
From: **Ayanna Bayo <ratlady@wz.org>**
Received: **Saturday, Oct. 18, 12:35 P.M.**
Subject: **Re: No Phone Calls**

Dear Frankie:

I promise not to tell your dad about our correspondence, if you promise to be honest with me from now on.

Honestly yours,

Ayanna

Saturday, October 18, 8:00 P.M.

Dear Diary:

Today I woke up early and e-mailed Rat-lady before anybody else was out of bed. The good news—miracle of miracles—is that Rat-lady promised not to tell Dad about the e-mails. The bad news is . . . where to start?

After e-mailing, I cocooned myself in a sleeping bag on the couch in the living room with a copy of *The Miracle Worker* to practice my lines. I tried to practice all the Annie Sulli-van lines, but Skip and Nutter were spying on me with Skip's camera and binoculars. They thought it was hilarious that I was talking to myself, so they secretly tape-recorded me and played it back very loudly. Ha-ha-ha.

Beth called, but I was too busy. Kept check-ing e-mail (and deleting Ratlady's messages to me so that Dad won't see them) and rehears-ing. After a while, I locked myself in my room and decided to work on the Helen Keller character, just in case. Helen Keller doesn't have any lines because she can't talk, so I put a paper grocery bag over my head and wandered around my room, feeling the darkness and the confusion and the fear. My room is small, so I opened my door and walked carefully down the stairs, gripping the banister dramatically. I'm quite sure nobody else in Maple County Junior High School is creative enough or dedicated enough to work this hard.

As I was walking between the kitchen and the living room, I heard some giggles, and I should have taken the bag off my head right then and there. But I was trying to feel deaf as well as blind, so I ignored the sounds and took another step, and tripped.

"Got ya, Baghead!" Skip yelled and laughed so hard his skinny arms and legs looked like they were going to fall apart.

It is impossible to be a serious actor while living in a zoo. Of course, because weekends are Dad's busiest time right now, I'm stuck at home with The Animals.

Dad came home at 6:30 in the best mood.

"I sold ten instruments today!" he sang as he walked in the door with a box. "And guess what?"

"You brought us presents?" Nutter asked.

"No, Mae brought this to the shop for Frankie." Dad pulled a devil's food cake out of the box. In blue frosting it read, HAPPY BIRTH-DAY, FRANKIE.

I thought: Boy, word sure travels fast here in Pepper Blossom, Indiana. But I didn't say anything.

"Mrs. Holmes told everybody it was Frankie's birthday yesterday," Dad said.

"Hurray!" Nutter exclaimed, and hopped on a stool to get a better look.

Dad looked at Skip and me. "Did one of you guys give her that idea?"

"I didn't!" Skip protested.

I shrugged as if I had no idea; but Dad looked like he really needed an explanation, so I added, "I'm pretty sure I heard that Mrs. Holmes has that disease that makes a person confused about things."

"Alzheimer's? Really? Where did you hear that?"

I was actually thinking about amnesia. But Alzheimer's, whatever that is, would work, too, so I nodded. "Remember when I went over to borrow the eggs last week? I heard her talking on the phone to her doctor. And then I saw the pills."

"Are you sure?"

I had to nod some more.

Dad sat down. "That's terrible. I should call her son in Indy and assure him that we'll keep an eye on her."

"No, you don't have to do that."

He shook his head. "It's a serious thing, Frankie. She must have a mild case, now, but it will probably get worse. Sometimes Alzheimer's patients get very confused and wander off."

"Mrs. Holmes hardly ever leaves her house," Skip said.

Dad laughed a little. "Well, that's true."

I jumped in. "I don't think she has the wandering kind of Alzheimer's. I think she has the kind that makes her confused about dates and people. The other day she thought Nutter was a puppy."

I swear I don't know where these ideas are coming from. I start with a kernel of an idea—like giving poor Mrs. Holmes a disease—and the next thing you know, she's confusing Nutter with a long lost puppy.

"Hey, Rover." Skip swatted Nutter on the head. Nutter, perfectly happy to be a puppy, sat on his hind legs and yapped.

Sunday, October 19, 10:00 P.M.

Dear Diary:

Oh, what a tangled web we weave when the telephone doth ring!

After church today Beth wanted to come over. I let her be Helen so I could practice Annie.

In the middle of my dramatic miracle-working, Bill Holmes called. He's the grown-up son of Mrs. Holmes. Dad must have called him about the Alzheimer's.

"Hi, Frankie. Is your Dad there?"

Thankfully he was not. He always opens Heartstrings right after church. "No, can I take a message?" I asked.

"Your dad left a message for me," he said. "Do you know why he called?"

"Oh, I think he meant to call *Dr.* Holmes. He's a new dentist. A special one that we have to take Skip to because his teeth are so crooked. . . ." (Skip heard that and punched me.) "My dad's been getting confused lately. Maybe he has Alzheimer's. . . ." Bill Holmes laughed. "I'll tell him you called, Mr. Holmes. If he doesn't call you back, you can assume it was just a mistake."

Not bad for thinking "on the fly," as Ms. Young used to say, although it cost me another buck to keep Skip quiet.

Beth wanted to know what was going on, so I explained about the birthday cake and the Alzheimer's. Then she drove me nuts because she acted like I was doomed to eternal flames for lying. "On top of all that, I can't believe you're going to forge a note!"

I said: "Why don't you just wear your choir robe all day long since you're such a goody-goody?"

She left in a huff.

There was one good thing: no messages or phone calls from Ratlady. My latest (and hopefully last) lie about the trailer must have done the trick.

After dinner the Red Beet Ramblers came over to rehearse. The Red Beet Ramblers is a group of a dozen people on dulcimer, guitar, fiddle, banjo, etc., who squash into our living room to play every Sunday evening. My mom and dad and their friend Ozzie Filmore started it before I was even born. I play certain songs with them on special occasions. We're doing "Give Me Your Hand" at the Fall Festival.

During rehearsal I tried not to think about any of my worries, and I just let the sound of my dulcimer and my voice melt into everybody else's. It was so beautiful I almost started to cry. Whenever the sixth-grade chorus would sing really well, Ms. Young used to always say: "Music has charms to soothe the savage beast." (It's really "savage breast." But the boys couldn't handle it when she said that, so she changed it to "beast.") Anyway, I think that's true about music.

This savage beast is hereby going to bed. I need my beauty sleep, for tomorrow is the big day. I want to look my best when everyone is congratulating me for getting the part of Annie Sullivan.

Monday, October 20, 3:15 p.m.

Dear Diary:

Days like this should be against the law.

First of all, I hate Mr. Justin Haxer. He didn't post the cast list until after school, so I had to wait all day. Ms. Young always posted the cast lists before school so you could see the results right away.

I had to start the day by bringing my forged note to the office. When I handed it to the secretary, my stomach was busy tying itself into a knot. All day I waited for The Troll to call my name over the intercom or to come and put me in handcuffs.

The last bell finally rang, and I thought I'd die before I could get to the drama room. A crowd was already pressing against the door where the list was posted. Melinda Bixby was squealing like a pig. I squeezed in.

Melinda got the part of Annie. Denise got the part of Helen. I was on the bottom of the list . . . as one of the "blind girls."

Denise and Melinda—both eighth-graders—were jumping up and down.

"Annie!" Denise cried.

"Helen!" Melinda cried.

They hugged and squealed. "This is going to be so much fun!" Melinda said.

"I knew you'd get the part," Denise cried.

The knot in my stomach felt like a dead reptile.

Me—a blind girl? The blind girls were only on for a few seconds in the very beginning of the play. They were little kids. They weren't important.

There were a few other seventh-graders standing around. "Congratulations, Frankie," Beth said. She never made anything but chorus, and this time she didn't make it at all. "You're so lucky."

I stared at her. Congratulations? For what? For being a blind girl? If she really was best-friend material she would be shouting at Mr. Horrible Haxer right now, telling him that the part of Annie Sullivan should have gone to me. What was wrong with him? Was *he* blind?

Mr. Haxer opened the door, and everybody started talking at once.

He made a few announcements, which I couldn't listen to because my entire being—including my eardrums—was filling up with hate for him.

He headed to the teachers' lounge, and I stopped him before I knew what I was going to say. And then it just came out: "I can't be in the play." I realized as soon as I said it that it was true. There was no way I could go to all those rehearsals and watch Melinda Bixby play the miracle worker.

"Why not?"

"My dad won't let me."

He looked puzzled and pulled me over to an empty part of the hallway where we could have some privacy. "Why? Is there a conflict with rehearsals?"

I nodded.

"What is it? Maybe we can work it out."

"No, I have to baby-sit my brothers after school every day."

"I'll talk with your dad. I'm sure—"

"No, don't!" That came out sounding a little panicky. So I added in a mature, perfectly Annie Sullivan voice, "I'm afraid that would be a tragic mistake, Mr. Haxer. He is under a lot of stress, and you shouldn't bother him." I should have stopped right there, but I'm like a freight train now—once I get started I'm hard to stop. "I'm afraid my dad is having a nervous breakdown."

Mr. Haxer looked shocked. "Oh Frankie, I'm so sorry to hear that." He touched my shoulder. Yesterday my heart would have melted under that touch. Now my heart was as cold and stiff as a garbage-can lid.

"How can we help?" he asked.

I stepped away. "He wouldn't want anybody to know. I'm just telling you because . . ."

He stepped closer and gave my shoulder a squeeze. "You should talk with Ms. Trolly, the guidance counselor, about all this, Frankie. That's what she's here for. She can—"

I pulled away. "No, I'm fine, thanks. I have to go now and pick up my brother."

I didn't start breathing until I got out the door.

The last part is true. I have to walk over to the elementary school to pick up Nutter. The only problem is that I have collapsed in a heap by my school's backdoor and I cannot get my legs to work. How can I possibly go on living?

7:55 P.M.

Life is cruel. I have locked myself in my room right now, and nobody cares. This whole thing with Ratlady is giving *me* a nervous breakdown. I don't know how I'm supposed to handle it when the rest of my life is falling apart. Not one single member of my so-called family asked me about the audition. Can you believe it?

I hate Ratlady. I hate my family. I hate junior high. I hate my life.

Here's what happened after my last entry.

I dragged myself over to the elementary school. As usual, Nutter was waiting for me by the flagpole, wearing that stupid koala backpack.

Skinny Skip ran past us without saying a word. He never waits for me and Nutter. He just runs as soon as the bell rings because he's now old enough to walk home by himself.

"Guess what I made today?" Nutter showed me a piece of black paper with a small white shape pasted on it. "Guess what it is?"

"I don't want to guess."

"I'll give you a clue. It mourns like this." He raised his arms and started moaning.

"It's a ghost. Ghosts don't mourn, Nutter. They moan."

Nutter had to run to catch up with me. "It's the best thing I've ever done. You can have it, Frankie."

"No thanks, Nutter."

"You're in a bad mood."

"Yep."

"How come?"

I pulled Nutter across the road, not saying anything.

"Well, I'm in a great mood." Nutter kept talking. "I figured out what I'm going to be for Halloween. I'm going to be a big daddy koala with lots of fur so I can carry my baby koala on my back."

"A big koala costume is too hard to make." I glanced at the picture he was holding. "You have to be something easy. Be a ghost."

"Dad can make me a koala costume."

"He's way too busy, Nutter. Stop focusing on that stupid koala backpack." We cut through the park, marching over the wooden bridge that goes over Dead Man's Creek. Nutter usually begs to stay and act out the Billy Goats Gruff or the Magic Fish story, but today he didn't say a word. I think he was afraid that if he did I'd bite his head off.

When we got home, Skip pounced. "Dad got a package from the zoo and so did you, Frankie." He held up two large, padded envelopes. "You got a book."

"Is there one for me?" Nutter asked.

"Nope," Skip said.

I grabbed both envelopes.

"Who's it from?" Nutter asked.

I looked at the package addressed to me. Sent Express Mail from the National Zoo in Washington, D.C., on Friday, October 17. Inside was a book about naked mole-rats.

Skip and Nutter stared at the picture on the cover. "What is it?" Nutter asked.

"It's the first-prize winner of the Ugliest Animal in the Universe," Skip said.

"Cool." Nutter grabbed the book.

"Check out those teeth!" Skip exclaimed. Then he read the small note stuck to the cover.

Dear Frankie:
   This book is for you and your brothers. I like reading as much as I like taking care of naked mole-rats. I hope you do, too.
   Nonfictionally yours,
   Ayanna

"Who's Ayanna?" Nutter asked.

"She's a mean rat lady who Dad met in Washington, D.C."

"She doesn't sound mean to me," Nutter said.

"She's a businesswoman or something," Skip said. "She's helping Dad to sell his stuff in Washington."

"What?"

Skip shrugged and pointed to the envelope addressed to Dad. "A good spy opens all mail."

Nutter opened the book to a picture of naked mole-rats rolling around in their own poop. "Look at this!"

While they dived into the book, I took Dad's envelope into my room and closed the door. The staples had already been taken out and new staples put in. Skip was pretty quick.

I took the staples out and opened the envelope. There were a bunch of pamphlets from the National Association of Musical Instrument Makers and a letter.

Dear Robert:

    Enclosed are the materials you accidentally left on the feeding-station cart in my office.

    After work today I stopped by that great music shop that I told you about (right around the corner from my apartment). They carry hammered and mountain dulcimers— none of which look as beautiful as the photos of yours that you showed me. I told them about your work, and they'd like you to contact them. I've included their card along with the pamphlets.

Fan-atically yours,
Ayanna

Skip thought she was a businesswoman. Wrong.

I could see it all now. Ratlady didn't care about business. She wanted Dad to move to Washington and sell his instruments at the music shop around the corner from her apartment so that she could be with him. I put the pamphlets back into the envelope and stapled it shut. No need for Dad to see the letter or the business card, so I pocketed those.

When Dad got home I expected him to ask me right away about the audition. But Skip and Nutter showed him the book from Ratlady, and he completely forgot about me.

"How nice." Dad flipped through the book.

"So, who's the person who sent it to us?" I asked innocently. I wanted to hear it from him.

"She's just a person who works at the zoo. She helped me pick out your souvenirs." He was trying to make it sound like she was some cashier or something.

"I like her already!" Nutter exclaimed, hugging the furry little head of his koala backpack. Then his eyes lit up. "Hey, I want to send her something." He ran to the kitchen and back. "See?" He held up his ghost picture.

"That's a stupid idea, Nutter," I said.

Nutter looked at me as if I'd shot him in the heart with a spear.

"It's a stupid idea because you gave the picture to me," I explained.

He scowled. "You didn't want it!"

Dad took the picture, ignoring me completely. "I'll send it as a thank-you card."

All through dinner I kept waiting for somebody to ask me about the audition. Nobody did. I swear I could be walking around with one leg chopped off and nobody would notice. After dinner Dad played poker with Skip and Nutter. I refused to play, and they all complained about what a bad mood I was in.

"She was in a bad mood when she picked me up at the flagpole," Nutter added.

"I'd be in a bad mood if I were her," Skip said.

"Why?" Dad asked.

"Because if I were Frankie, I'd be as ugly as a naked mole-rat!"

They all laughed.

"You think that's funny?" I yelled. "If I said that to Skip, I'd get grounded."

Dad waved it off. "Skip wasn't serious, Frankie. It was just a joke."

"I hate this whole family!" I yelled, and locked myself in my room.

Of course they let me go. They just kept playing their happy game. Who cares about Frankie? Who cares if Frankie ever comes out of her room again? The house is better off without her.

Here I sit. Here I will rot.

Things are even worse.

About fifteen minutes ago the phone rang.

I thought about who it could be. Ratlady? The Troll? Mr. Haxer? The volunteer fire department wishing me a happy birthday?

"Frankie," Dad called, "it's Beth."

"I don't want to talk. I have to work on a stupid science report."

He must have hung up because after a few minutes the phone rang again. This time he didn't call for me. I crept out the door. Quietly I picked up the other phone. I recognized the voice immediately. It was a beautiful voice from the past: Ms. Young.

"Do you have a minute to talk about the play, Robert?"

"What play?"

"The junior high school play . . ."

Mr. Horrible Haxer must have told Ms. Young about Dad having a nervous breakdown. I could hear it in her voice; it had that careful sound that people use when they're talking to sick people. What would she do? Would she tell Dad that she knew about his nervous breakdown? I cupped my hand over the receiver so they couldn't hear me breathing.

"I wanted Frankie to know how proud I was that she got cast," Ms. Young went on. "Seventh-graders rarely get in."

"I forgot about the play!" Dad said. "She didn't even tell me she got in. How nice of you to call. It'll mean a lot to her. You were her favorite teacher, you know."

"Well, I'm a little worried about . . ." She didn't know what to say. Please don't say anything about a nervous breakdown, I prayed. "I was wondering if there was any way to make it work so that Frankie could be in the show. I think it would be very good for her."

"Of course she can be in the play."

"She can? You're sure it's not too much trouble for you to arrange? Frankie told Justin Haxer that you needed her to baby-sit every day after school. And if you need some help working that out, I'm sure . . ."

Justin, I thought. Ms. Young should know that his real name is Horrible.

"I know how important these school plays are to Frankie," Dad was saying. "Of course we'll work things out here."

"Oh, I'm so glad to hear that. May I speak with Frankie?"

I hung up the phone and ran into my room.

"Frankie!" Dad called up the stairs. "Ms. Young wants to talk to you."

"I can't talk right now," I yelled back.

I waited a few seconds; then I crept back out and picked up the phone.

"Sure," Dad was saying. "We'll talk it over. How many rehearsals a week?"

"Justin will write up a rehearsal schedule. It won't be that many. She has a very small part. I'm glad you don't feel overwhelmed by this."

"Overwhelmed? Why should I feel over-whelmed?"

"I really didn't want to bother you, but I can't help feeling that it's important for Frankie to participate."

"No, I'm glad you called. I can arrange baby-sitting."

"Great! I'll tell Justin."

As they said their good-byes, I hung up and ran into my room.

A few minutes later I heard Dad's footsteps on the stairs. He knocked and waited. When I didn't say anything, he knocked again.

I put my pillow over my head. "I can't talk right now."

"That was Ms. Young on the phone. She said you got in—"

"I know."

"Frankie, you can be in the play. You know that. Why did you tell Mr. Haxer that you couldn't?"

"I don't want to be in the play."

"What?"

"I already told Mr. Haxer that I'm not doing it. So just stay out of it."

"I don't understand. Open the door, Frankie."

I didn't move.

"Can we please talk about his face to face?"

I threw my pillow at the door. "Why? You don't care."

"Don't snap at me, Frankie. I do care. I'm trying to help."

"Well you can help by leaving me alone."

There was silence again. He didn't know what to do. If I was a dad, and I had forgotten to ask my daughter about an audition, and my daughter was this upset, I wouldn't leave her alone. I'd cut a hole through the door, or I'd get a ladder and climb through the window. I'd think of a million and one ways of finding out what was wrong and cheering her up.

He cleared his throat, something he does when he doesn't know what to say. "I don't get it, Frankie. What's going on?" he finally asked.

I didn't answer.

"Of course you don't have to be in the play if you don't want to be. But I don't understand why you don't want to be. Let's talk about it." He waited for a response. After a minute he said, "Well, I'm going to tuck Nutter in, and then I'll be downstairs if you want to talk about it."

His footsteps thudded down the hall.

I picked up the copy of *The Miracle Worker* from the library and threw it at the door. Then I picked it up again, and I watched myself tear out page after page after page. I'm not really doing this, I thought, but I really was. Why did Ms. Young have to call? I hate her and Mr. Haxer and Dad and Melinda and Denise and everybody. Even Beth.

9:15 P.M.

I have to write again. Here's what just happened. After I desicrated (desecrated? decimated? deseminated?) the stupid book and poured my heart out in these pages (crying all the while), I heard a little scratch at the door. Right away I knew it wasn't Dad.

"Frankie!" It was Nutter's whisper. Then a piece of paper slipped under the door.

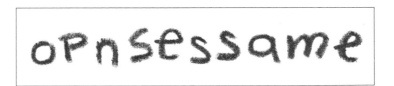

"It's a magic word," Nutter whispered. "You have to open up."

I opened the door a crack. Nutter slipped in, his eyes drawn to the crime scene on the floor. "This is bad," he whispered.

I sat on my bed. "I know."

He climbed up beside me and just sat there, next to me. I felt like I was going to cry again if I looked at him or talked to him, so I stared at the back cover of *The Miracle Worker*. Then something brushed my shoulders, and I turned to see that he was trying to put his koala's furry arms around my back. Nutter's face was so close to mine, all I could see was his big chocolate eyes through my tears.

He whispered, "You can sleep with him tonight."

My throat closed up and I felt like I couldn't breathe.

"That's okay, Nutter," I managed to say. "You sleep with him. Come on; it's way past your bedtime. I'll tuck you in."

I opened the door and Skip tumbled in, his camera and night-vision binoculars flashing.

"Hey," Nutter yelped. "You were spying on us!"

"Got ya!" Skip yelled, and ran. Nutter chased him, and I chased them both.

How can something make you feel better and make you cry harder at the same time? Nutter's little face up close to mine made me feel better, but it also made me miss Mom more somehow. She died so long ago, I bet Nutter doesn't even remember her. That just isn't right. And it isn't right that Nutter and Skip and I have to cheer each other up. She should be the one cheering us up. If she were here, she would have asked me right away how the audition was. Why can't she just come back?

10:30 P.M.

I'm going to bed now. Dad just knocked on the door again. He made me unlock it because he said it wasn't safe to sleep with a locked door in case of fire. I unlocked it, but I wouldn't open it. I can't talk to him about anything.

Tuesday, October 21, 2:15 P.M.

Dear Diary:

I'm in the nurse's office with a debilitating headache. Even my eyes hurt. Annie Sullivan's eyes hurt often. I can't remember why. Maybe it was stress. It is yet another reason why I should have gotten the part; I can *relate.* I bet Melinda Bixby's eyes have never hurt.

Even though I am in pain, I will write down the story of my day. Another horrible day, of course. How many horrible days can a person endure? This one started at dawn.

When I woke, what lovely sight greeted me? The rosy glow of the sun? A merry robin chirping outside my window? No. The gruesome murder of an innocent book. The evidence was glaring at me: one hundred twenty-two poor pages. Ripped. Separated. Dead. And I am the murderer. Why did I do it? Why can't I control myself?

I hid the pages in an empty tissue box and hurried down to breakfast. I expected—I don't know—a little sympathy, perhaps, for not getting the part I wanted? But everybody just jumped on me for waking up so late.

"Hurray! Her Majesty finally woke up," Dad said, and handed me a cereal box as if it were a box of frankincense and merr (myrr? myrrh?).

I shot him one of my fiercest looks and headed for the fridge.

"It was a joke, Frankie," Dad said. "I was hoping you'd be in a better mood today than yesterday."

"Me too," Skip added, shoveling cereal into his mouth straight from the box. How does he stay so skinny when he eats like a pig?

Nutter hugged me from the back. "Dad said *you'd* make me a big koala costume, Frankie."

"No way."

"You said last week you wanted to be a ghost, Nutter," Skip said.

"I'm done being a ghost," Nutter said.

"But you haven't even been a ghost yet!" I argued.

"Come on, Frankie." Dad poured coffee into his Thermos. "He wants to be a koala.

I'm really pressed for time. I got in a big order that I want to do a really good job on."

"I'm pressed for time, too."

"You are not," Skip said. "I heard you say you're not going to do the play."

"Actually," Dad said, "I was hoping we could talk some more about that, Frankie. I really think you should be in the play. We'll talk about it tonight, okay?"

I didn't say anything. My eyes had become fixated on a large envelope on the counter with Ratlady's name. "Do you want me to drop this off at the post office?" I asked. The P.O. is right next to my school.

"That would be great, thanks!"

"Is that my ghost for Ayanna?" Nutter asked, grabbing the envelope.

"Just like I promised." Dad took it back from Nutter and handed it to me.

As I walked the boys to the elementary school, Agent Skip Wallop suggested that we open the envelope and see if Dad wrote a letter.

I pretended to be disgusted by the idea. I feel a need to protect Skip and Nutter. I think if they were to read a love letter from Dad, they might go into shock. "Correspondence between two people should be private," I said. I dropped them off and cut across the field toward my school. Of course when I passed the post office, I "forgot" to mail the envelope.

Beth was waiting for me at the front door. She had already heard that I had said no to Mr. Haxer, and she thought I was crazy. That's because she isn't accustomed to being a star. She'd probably be delighted to play the part of a tree.

First period Mr. Horrible Haxer got on the intercom and said that any copies of *The Miracle Worker* that were checked out of the library needed to be turned in so that the actors who have lines could use them.

"Mr. Peter?" Beth raised her hand. "Frankie and I both checked out copies. Can we go to the library and return them?"

Thanks a lot, Beth, I thought. I imagined handing the librarian the tissue-box coffin filled with lifeless pages.

"No, you cannot," Mr. Peter said. "We have a review to get through. The test is tomorrow."

For once I liked Mr. Battery-Operated Peter.

After the review, he gave us time to study for the test. I propped my book on my desk and opened the envelope addressed to Ratlady. There was Nutter's ghost picture. I remember Nutter saying that it was the best thing he'd ever done, so I looked at it.

The torn white shape against the black background really looked like a little ghost. The arms and eyes were raised up sadly, as if he were moaning, calling for another ghost maybe; and yet the sky all around him was empty and black. The ghost looked so little and lonely that it brought a quick rush of sadness into my throat.

It seemed like a private thing—this picture. I hated the thought of Ratlady receiving it. What would she see? A torn piece of white paper stuck on black paper with clumpy glue? Would she think it was cute? Would she laugh and throw it away?

A letter addressed to Ratlady in Dad's handwriting was paper-clipped to the back. I slipped Nutter's picture into my binder and read the letter.

Dear Ayanna,

Thanks again for sending the book to my kids. Nutter wanted you to have this picture. It's a ghost.

He is very excited about Halloween and wants to be a daddy koala so that he can carry around his baby koala (the backpack). He said he likes you already.

And the answer to our last question is no! Your e-mails to Heartstrings haven't been distracting me from my work; they've been inspiring me. After your first reply on Saturday, I sat down and played like I haven't played in years. There was a newly married couple in the shop and when I was done, they bought the dulcimer right out from under my fingers.

You're like the sun coming up in the morning, Ayanna. Everything about you shines with warmth and light. Even your e-mails.

How can I feel this close to you when we've just met? How can I feel this close to you when you live so far away?

Wanting to see you again,
Robert
P.S. Look for a box in the mail soon.

E-mails to the shop? What a dirty rat. She was using his business e-mail address so that I couldn't read their messages. And since when did he like e-mailing? I ripped the letter in half, and Mr. Peter looked up from his desk. "You're making a lot of noise, Frankie. Do you need any help?"

"No, thank you." I stuffed the pieces into my backpack and got out a blank sheet of paper. I knew I needed to get some problems done in case Mr. Peter decided to roam the rows. But the torn halves of the letter seemed to be shouting at me from the depths of my backpack, *Dad and Ratlady are falling in love!* How could I review for a test when the Big Bang of bad news was exploding in my brain?

I couldn't stop thinking about the consequences. If they got married, would we move there or would she move in with us? I imagined our house. When other people see our house, they probably just see a messy place with lots of wood and odd things everywhere. The wood is Dad because he is a great carpenter and, of course, dulcimer-maker. We have wood floors. Big wooden bookcases. Dulcimers hanging on all the walls. The odd things are Mom. She hung a red chair from the ceiling in the living room so that it looks like it's floating in air. She wallpapered the kitchen with postcards of the world's most beautiful places, even though Grandpa Ted said you can't wallpaper a room with postcards. She lackered (laquered? lacquered?) old family photographs onto the dining room table so that we'd always be eating with the whole family. She sewed brightly colored fringe onto all our pillowcases so that we'd have wild dreams.

I pictured Ratlady driving up with a moving van. She'd probably want to throw out the chair, rip down the postcards, and hang up pictures of naked mole-rats. She'd probably make us sleep on boring white pillowcases. She'd probably arrive with her own furniture, all coated with the smell of small mammals.

Or what if we had to move to Washington, D.C.? I've seen pictures. It's all concrete. No trees. No creek. Kids take subways to school and get mugged on the playground. I wouldn't know anybody there but Ratlady!

How could any normal dad fall in love with a stranger? Who was this Ratlady, really? What kind of person would fall in love with a guy who has:

1. Two sons who drool and have diarrhea?
2. A nose that is always full of snot because he is allergic to many things, including small mammals?
3. A tendency to say ridiculous things because of a special drug that he is on?
4. No money?
5. A crowded trailer to live in?

The lies that I've been telling her obviously haven't been working. Could it be because she's a good person who doesn't really care about drooling or money or snotty noses? There must be something that would turn her off. What would turn off a really good person? I wanted to figure this out, but I kept getting interrupted.

I managed to get through the rest of the day by looking interested in my teachers. It's called acting, and I am very good at it, which is why I should have been given the role of Annie Sullivan.

P.S. At lunch I had a fight with Beth. She told me that she signed up for stage crew. I can't believe it. Why would anyone want to be involved in a play with Melinda Bixby as the lead? Beth said she thought it would be "fun" and "educational" and a way to get on Mr. Haxer's "good side." I felt like handing her my fork and saying, Go ahead; stab my heart. She doesn't get it.

3:15 P.M.

Mr. Horrible Haxer just ran into me in the hall.

"Good news, Frankie," he said. "I hear that it's okay with your dad for you to be in the play. Come to my room to pick up the rehearsal schedule. The librarian said you already have a script, right?"

I shifted my backpack. "I can't come. If my father told you I can come it's because he's ashamed of his condition. He doesn't want people knowing that he is having a nervous breakdown, which is why it wasn't very nice of you to tell Ms. Young."

Mr. Haxer's horribly handsome face turned as red as a baboon's butt. "I only mentioned your situation to Ms. Young because she cares so much about you, and—"

I took off down the hall before he could say more.

Trying to get out of the play and keep Dad and Ratlady apart is a full-time job. As soon as I get home, I'm going to take care of things once and for all. I know I said that I wasn't going to lie anymore, but that was before finding out that they're carrying on a secret correspondence at Heartstrings. I have thought of something that will definitely work on The Rat. This will be the last lie.

Over and out.

To: **Ayanna Bayo <ratlady@wz.org>**
From: **Robert Wallop <wallop@dman.com>**
Sent: **Tuesday, Oct. 21, 3:45 P.M.**
Subject: **Serious News**

Ms. Bayo:

There is news that I thought you should know about. My father is going to get married again. The wedding date is set for Thanksgiving Day because we are all so very thankful.

She is a beautiful young woman who has many talents. The only problem is that the special drugs my father is taking sometimes confuse him. He says (and writes) things to other women, thinking that he is really saying (or writing) them to her. So if my father should ever say (or write) anything romantic to you, please ignore him for the sake of his fiancée.

You are obviously a good person. I'm sure you will do the right thing.

Helpfully yours,

Frankie

To: **Robert Wallop <wallop@dman.com>**
From: **Ayanna Bayo <ratlady@wz.org>**
Received: **Tuesday, Oct. 21, 5:00 P.M.**
Subject: **To Frankie**

Dear Frankie:

Your father didn't mention anything about a fiancée, and he certainly doesn't seem like the kind of man to keep secrets. I can't help wondering if you are making up things to put me off.

Can you talk to your dad about your feelings?

Ayanna

To: **Ayanna Bayo <ratlady@wz.org>**
From: **Robert Wallop <wallop@dman.com>**
Sent: **Tuesday, Oct. 21, 5:10 P.M.**
Subject: **No!**

Ms. Bayo:

I am angry and a palled by the fact that you don't believe me. What does it take? I guess you need evidence.

No, I can't talk to my dad about my feelings.
My dad and I don't talk about anything.
   Frankie

To: **Robert Wallop <wallop@dman.com>**
From: **Ayanna Bayo <ratlady@wz.org>**
Received: **Tuesday, Oct. 21, 5:30 P.M.**
Subject: **Honesty**

Dear Frankie:
   I'm sorry that you are appalled by my
suggestion that you created a fictional fiancée to
put me off. I wanted to be honest with you about
what I was thinking. I want you to be honest with
me, too.
   People can get into the habit of hiding their true
feelings or not talking to each other. And habits are
hard to break.
   This reminds me of a funny thing that happened
today. While all the mole-rats were huddled in their
nest, I closed the nest off so that they couldn't get
out. Then I changed the direction of one part of the
tunnel system. For weeks there has been a long
section of straight tubing coming from the nest. But

this morning I took out the straight tubing and replaced it with a section that has several sharp turns.

When I opened the "door" to the nest, the queen nudged three large workers out to investigate. They scampered out the door, as always, in a single-file line and with their eyes closed. The first mole-rat in line scampered down the tunnel and when he came to the new section, instead of following the new tunnel as it turned to the right, he tried to keep going straight—out of habit—and bumped into the wall! The other mole-rats bumped into him.

The amazing thing about mole-rats is that they make new habits quickly. I collected the three little stooges and put them back into the nest. When they came out again, they didn't make the same mistake.

Maybe you and your dad have gotten into the habit of not talking to each other. Maybe you could both break the habit?

Habitually yours,
Ayanna

To: Ayanna Bayo <ratlady@wz.org>
From: Robert Wallop <wallop@dman.com>
Sent: Tuesday, Oct. 21, 5:47 P.M.
Subject: Re: Honesty

Dear Ms. Bayo:

I think it was mean of you to lock the mole-rats in their nest, change their tunnel, and then watch them bump into a wall. Did you ever consider that maybe the naked mole-rats liked their tunnel the way it was? Did you ever consider that they might not like someone sticking her fingers in and changing things? I think the queen should decide when and if changes are made to a tunnel system. If I were queen, I wouldn't make any changes. Change is bad.

Concerned,

Frankie

To: Robert Wallop <wallop@dman.com>
From: Ayanna Bayo <ratlady@wz.org>
Received: Tuesday, Oct. 21, 5:53 P.M.
Subject: Change Can Be Good

Dear Frankie:

I didn't change the tunnel system for my amusement. I did it to keep the mole-rats active and challenged. A good keeper doesn't take care of her animals just by feeding them and keeping their exhibits clean. A good keeper tries to re-create some of the conditions and experiences the animals would have in the wild.

In the wild the tunnels of naked mole-rats sometimes cave in or get plugged up. So from time to time I interfere. I try to change things in ways that mimic what might happen to a mole-rat colony in the wild. That way the animals are able to respond appropriately. Change can be good! Change helps you to grow.

I do understand and share your concern. Some people do not like zoos because they believe no animals should be held captive. I believe that a good zoo is an educational institution where biologists study animals and people get the chance to see them. People can learn to respect and care about animals and their habitats by visiting exhibits in zoos like mine. If animals are well treated and given an environment that is as close as possible to their native habitat, then the animals can live healthy lives and help the world to be a better place. Sometimes we reintroduce animals that have been bred in captivity back into the wild. That's always especially thrilling for a keeper.

For me, being a keeper is an awesome responsibility. I know these mole-rats, and I think they know that I'm *for* them. (At least they know my smell!) The colony is very healthy and has lived a long time. The queen is pregnant again now.

Thoughtfully yours,

Ayanna

To: **Ayanna Bayo <ratlady@wz.org>**
From: **Robert Wallop <wallop@dman.com>**
Sent: **Tuesday, Oct. 21, 5:59 P.M.**
Subject: **Re: Change Can Be Good**

Dear Ms. Bayo:

If naked mole-rats could talk, would you ask them if they liked being held captive at the zoo? What if they said no?

—F.

To: **Robert Wallop <wallop@dman.com>**
From: **Ayanna Bayo <ratlady@wz.org>**
Received: **Tuesday, Oct. 21, 6:03 P.M.**
Subject: **Re: Change Can Be Good**

Dear Frankie:

You ask thought-provoking questions. If naked mole-rats could talk, I certainly wouldn't keep them cooped up in a plastic tunnel system.

Honestly yours,

Ayanna

To: **Ayanna Bayo <ratlady@wz.org>**
From: **Robert Wallop <wallop@dman.com>**
Sent: **Tuesday, Oct. 21, 6:05 P.M.**
Subject: **Rights**

Dear Ms. Bayo:

So you think it's okay to imprison creatures because they can't talk back? I don't think anything should be imprisoned. It reminds me of the way grown-ups control the lives of kids. Kids and naked mole-rats should have more rights.

If I were a naked mole-rat, I wouldn't want to be moved from Africa. Nobody should take anybody away from home. Ever.
Sincerely,
Frankie

To: **Robert Wallop <wallop@dman.com>**
From: **Ayanna Bayo <ratlady@wz.org>**
Received: **Tuesday, Oct. 21, 6:11 P.M.**
Subject: **Re: Rights**

Dear Frankie:
    I certainly agree that kids, naked mole-rats, and all creatures should be treated with respect and dignity. I am a vegetarian because I don't like the way that animals are treated by large-scale agribusiness companies.
    But there are times when adults need to intervene in the lives of creatures—or kids—to protect them and help them to grow up.
    If koalas were about to become extinct, wouldn't it be better for a biologist to capture several and keep them protected in a zoo, hoping that they will mate and have babies, rather than

letting them become extinct? Should koalas have the *right* to become extinct?

What kind of rights should kids have? Should twelve-year-old boys and girls be allowed to drive cars if they want to? Should kids be able to decide whether or not they want to go to school? Should kids be able to baby-sit themselves? At what age?

Philosophically yours,
Ayanna

To: **Ayanna Bayo <ratlady@wz.org>**
From: **Robert Wallop <wallop@dman.com>**
Sent: **Tuesday, Oct. 21, 6:12 P.M.**
Subject: **Questions**

Dear Ms. Bayo:

I didn't like any of your questions. I thought they were smart-alecky. Obviously kids like Nutter should not be allowed to drive. What I mean is that adults should ask kids for their opinions before they make decisions about them.

Opinionatedly yours,
Frankie

To: **Robert Wallop <wallop@dman.com>**
From: **Ayanna Bayo <ratlady@wz.org>**
Received: **Tuesday, Oct. 21, 6:14 P.M.**
Subject: **Re: Questions**

Dear Frankie:

Well said. I think it's great that you are thinking about these philosophical questions and are developing opinions of your own. Exercise your brain!

Ayanna

To: **Ayanna Bayo <ratlady@wz.org>**
From: **Robert Wallop <wallop@dman.com>**
Sent: **Tuesday, Oct. 21, 6:16 P.M.**
Subject: **Re: Questions**

Dear Ms. Bayo:

Now I have a question for you. If I am telling the truth and my dad really is getting married to somebody else, will you leave him alone?

Curiously yours,

Frankie

To: Robert Wallop <wallop@dman.com>
From: Ayanna Bayo <ratlady@wz.org>
Received: Tuesday, Oct. 21, 6:18 P.M.
Subject: Re: Questions

Dear Frankie:

I think your father is a wonderful man who deserves all the love in the world. If he found someone to love, someone who truly loved him in return, then I'd be happy for him.

Yours truly,

Ayanna

P.S. Your dad mentioned that you decided not to be in the play—I'm sorry about that.

To: Ayanna Bayo <ratlady@wz.org>
From: Robert Wallop <wallop@dman.com>
Sent: Tuesday, Oct. 21, 6:19 P.M.
Subject: Re: Questions

Why is everybody so sorry that I'm not in the stupid play?

To: Robert Wallop <wallop@dman.com>
From: Ayanna Bayo <ratlady@wz.org>
Received: Tuesday, Oct. 21, 6:29 p.m.
Subject: Re: Questions

Dear Frankie:

I can't answer for everybody. I can only answer for myself. I'm sorry because I think being in a play is a great opportunity. Being a part of a production is a cooperative experience: all the people—the actors, the director, and the stagehands—are working together to create something meaningful. No one person could do it alone. Everyone is needed, no matter how small the part.

I think there should be more cooperative projects in the world. It used to be that everyone in a village helped one another to build houses and grow food and take care of children. Now we are all isolated. We cook in our own separate kitchens, drive our separate cars, and work in our separate offices. I have lived in my apartment for three years, and I don't know many of my neighbors. There's something wrong with that.

If a naked mole-rat tried to live alone, it would

starve. The ground is hard, so it takes a whole colony working together to dig far enough to find food.

Remember how I told you I try to keep the mole-rats active by re-creating the challenges they experience in their natural habitat? In the wild, naked mole-rats dig through the hard ground until they run into a "root" vegetable. Once they've chomped through that veggie, they have to dig through the hard dirt until they bump into another root or bulb. So here's what I do: From time to time I plug up one of their tunnels with about six inches of very hard dirt. At the end I stick in half a sweet potato or an ear of corn, as if it has grown in the dirt beyond their existing tunnel. As soon as I get done packing in the dirt with the food at the end, a few mole-rats scurry down the other end of the tunnel to investigate. Soon, they form an assembly line for digging. It's so much fun to watch. They form a single-file line with a "digger" mole-rat in the front, followed by a line of "sweeper" mole rats. The digger chews the dirt with his or her long teeth and brushes the dirt under his or her legs. The sweeper directly behind him or her collects the dirt into a pile and scuttles backward with it, brushing the dirt back with him or her. The funny thing is that all the rest of the mole-rats in the line rise up on their tiptoes so that the sweeper can go backward under their arms and legs. The digger keeps working and passes more dirt to the next sweeper in line, who takes that little pile all the way to the back of the line. It looks like a game that children might play, but really it's a lot of work. One animal could never do it alone. They depend on one another.

I hope that you will audition for the next play.

Dramatically yours,

Ayanna

To: Ayanna Bayo <ratlady@wz.org>
From: Robert Wallop <wallop@dman.com>
Sent: Tuesday, Oct. 21, 6:30 P.M.
Subject: Independence

A.:

I'm glad I am not a naked mole-rat. I am independent. I am proud of being able to take care of myself. I don't need anybody, and that's the way I like it.

—F.

To: **Robert Wallop <wallop@dman.com>**
From: **Ayanna Bayo <ratlady@wz.org>**
Received: **Tuesday, Oct. 21, 6:31 P.M.**
Subject: **Re: Independence**

Dear F.:

I admire your spirit. You are independent, but you aren't alone. You are a part of a family. Your brothers depend on you. I think it is good to be needed. Being needed can keep an independent person balanced.

I am independent, too. But other than my naked mole-rats, nobody really needs me, and that makes me feel lonely sometimes. I spend way too much time on the computer.

Yours,

A.

To: Ayanna Bayo <ratlady@wz.org>
From: Robert Wallop <wallop@dman.com>
Sent: Tuesday, Oct. 21, 6:32 P.M.
Subject: Re: Independence

Why doesn't anybody need you? Don't you have any family?

To: Robert Wallop <wallop@dman.com>
From: Ayanna Bayo <ratlady@wz.org>
Received: Tuesday, Oct. 21, 6:35 P.M.
Subject: Re: Independence

Dear Frankie:

I don't have any brothers or sisters. My parents have both passed away. I have several aunts and uncles and many cousins, but they live in either New York or Kenya. I do enjoy working with my colleagues at the zoo, and I love talking with all the children who visit the naked mole-rat exhibit.

We're having a big party here on Halloween called "The Zoo Boo." All the people who work at the zoo hand out treats to the visitors. It's my favorite day of the year.

I think you are lucky to have Skip and Nutter and your dad. From the way your dad has talked about Pepper Blossom, it sounds like the kind of village where everybody looks out for everybody else. I think that sounds nice.

—A.

P.S. Are you looking forward to Halloween? What's your costume?

To:　　**Ayanna Bayo <ratlady@wz.org>**
From:　　**Robert Wallop <wallop@dman.com>**
Sent:　　**Tuesday, Oct. 21, 6:37 P.M.**
Subject:　**Halloween**

I am too old for Halloween. I have to make Nutter a koala costume. Skip is dressing up as a spy, which is not a costume because he really is one.

—F.

To: Robert Wallop <wallop@dman.com>
From: Ayanna Bayo <ratlady@wz.org>
Received: Tuesday, Oct. 21, 6:38 P.M.
Subject: Re: Halloween

I might be too old to dress up, but I'm doing it anyway. I love costumes.
—A.

To: Ayanna Bayo <ratlady@wz.org>
From: Robert Wallop <wallop@dman.com>
Sent: Tuesday, Oct. 21, 6:39 P.M.
Subject: Re: Halloween

Let me guess. You're going as a naked mole-rat.
—F.

To: Robert Wallop <wallop@dman.com>
From: Ayanna Bayo <ratlady@wz.org>
Received: Tuesday, Oct. 21, 6:48 P.M.
Subject: Re: Halloween

Ha! No, I'm not going as a naked mole-rat. I am going as a giraffe this year. I'm making a fun costume—did I mention that I make costumes and masks? I have quite a collection. One of the local children's theater companies often asks me to make things for their productions. Here's a scanned sketch of my giraffe headdress:

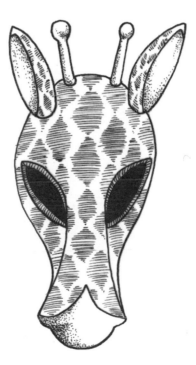

Anyway I'm tall and skinny, so I think I'll make a good giraffe. I'll be the only tall mammal in the small mammal house. Ha-ha. I need to go now. Nice "talking" with you.

    —A.

Still Tuesday, 8:10 P.M.

What goes on in our house is more dramatic than anything you could possibly see on stage or screen. Although I am hungry enough to gnaw off my own right arm, I'm going to refrain so that I can write down everything that has happened since 3:00 P.M.

The first thing I did when I got home from school was send an e-mail to Ratlady, informing her that Dad is getting married again. Brilliant, eh? I thought the lie would stop her in her little ratty tracks. But she didn't believe me, and somehow we got off track. She is highly effective at going off track. I need to figure out a way to stay on track and convince her.

I have to admit that there is one good thing about Ratlady: She doesn't talk down to me.

Dad came home late and brought a chicken potpie from Mae's, which I could smell the minute he walked in the door. I did not relish the idea of sitting down to dinner with Skip the Spy, Nutter the Koala-wannabe, and Dad the wild shirt–wearing lover boy, who is carrying on a secret correspondence when he should be working. But I was starved, and I love Mae's chicken potpie: all golden and bubbly under the crisp crust.

Dad also brought home the pieces of a new dulcimer to work on after dinner. He never does that, and it made me wonder. Did he bring it home because he was too busy e-mailing Ratlady to get his work done during the day? Or did he bring it home because it's a special dulcimer that he's making for someone special? On the phone he had been trying to talk Ratlady into playing. And in his note he had said that she should expect a box in the mail. Could he be making a dulcimer for her?

The thought of him giving a dulcimer to her made me really angry. He and Mom played together. He shouldn't be playing with anybody else.

All these thoughts were bubbling under the crisp crust of my brain as we sat down to dinner. Dad dished up big helpings of potpie to everybody, and Nutter's face scrunched up like he was about to vomit. "I hate chicken pie," he complained.

"Well it's what we're having for dinner. So dig in," Dad said with a big smile. He clearly didn't care.

"Well I'm not eating." Nutter crossed his arms.

"Fine."

Nutter started to cry. "You *want* me to starve?"

Dad ignored him. "Skip, it's your turn to wash the dishes tonight. After dinner I need to spend some time working in the basement. I'm making a masterpiece."

"So who's the new dulcimer for?" I asked very casually.

He took a swig of water. "Nobody special. I'm just experimenting with a new design idea."

Liar, I wanted to say. I stuck my fork into a chunk of white meat.

Dad asked Skip how school was. While Skip chattered on about what he saw in his teacher's desk drawer, I stared at the square of chicken on my fork. Normally I would pop it into my mouth, but tonight I couldn't. Every time I looked at the little piece, I kept seeing a live chicken staring back at me. How could somebody chop up a live chicken and bake it in a pie?

I pushed my plate away.

"Frankie—why aren't you eating?"

"I can't eat it," I said. "I'm a vegetarian."

Dad dropped his fork. "Since when?"

"Since now."

He shook his head like he wanted to stick us in a box and ship us to China. "Two out of three not eating. You guys have no idea how annoying you can be."

"What's wrong with being a vegetarian?" I asked. Your darling Ayanna Bayo is a vegetarian, I wanted to say, and I bet you don't yell at her for it.

Nutter wailed. "I'm not annoying. I'm starving. Nobody cares that I'm starving?"

"You can't starve, Nutter," Skip said. "You

ate the rest of Frankie's birthday cake right before dinner."

Instead of getting mad at Nutter for eating the cake, or at Skip for tattling, Dad turned his attention to me. "Frankie, why on earth did you let Nutter have cake before dinner?"

"I didn't give it to him."

"Aren't you supposed to be watching him after school?"

Nutter sniffled and hugged his koala backpack to his chest. "She's *supposed* to make me a koala costume, and all she did was e-mail."

"She was e-mailing Ayanna Bayo," Skip blurted out.

The truth came flying at me like an ice ball in the face. "You skinny little creep!" I shrieked, and threw down my fork. It bounced off the table and almost hit Skip.

My anger shut up everybody for a second. Then Dad's voice became as tight and thin as a wire. "Frankie, that is way out of line."

"Why don't you tell Skip to mind his own business? Why don't you tell Nutter to stop being such a baby?"

Nutter ran from the table.

I got up, and Dad grabbed my hand.

"Sit down," he said.

"Forget it." I pulled away.

"Don't talk to me like that, Frankie."

"What are you going to do? Nail me to the chair? You don't care about me anyway." I ran up to my room and locked the door.

He pounded up the stairs and knocked. "Frankie, you can't keep locking yourself in there."

"Why should I talk when all you do is yell at me?"

"What's this about e-mailing the woman from the zoo?"

"Nothing. I had some questions about her stupid naked mole-rats. That's all. She sent her e-mail address with that book and said if I had any questions, I should e-mail her. Is that a crime?"

He was silent. With any luck, he'd believe me.

Nutter's voice came through. "Is that naked rat lady coming here?"

"Nutter, I'm talking to Frankie now. Okay? Frankie, will you please open the door? This is ridiculous."

Nutter wailed. "Nobody cares about me."

I could hear in Dad's voice that he was struggling to be patient. "That's not true. Blow your nose, Nutter."

There were some sounds of rustling and mumbling outside my door. I looked around my room. The tissue box full of *The Miracle Worker* pages was gone.

I pressed my ear against the door and heard the unmistakable sound of dead pages being pulled from a box. "Frankie." Dad's voice collapsed. "What in the world . . . Oh Frankie, how could you destroy a book like this?"

From the bottom of the stairs, Skip yelled, "She did it last night."

I slammed my hand against the door. "Would you stop spying on me!"

Through the door I heard Dad send Skip and Nutter to their room.

I paced. The best thing to do would be to confess to the murder of the book and apologize. But I find it very hard to admit that I'm wrong. There's something about Dad's voice. When he's disappointed or angry, his voice comes at me like warm mud and clogs up my brain.

"Frankie, I think I know the reason you don't want to be in the play," he went on. "Skip said that you practiced very hard for the leading role, and my guess is that you are disappointed that you didn't get the part. I understand your disappointment, but I still think it would be good experience for you to be in the play. In elementary school you were a big fish in a little pond, Frankie. Now that you're in junior high school, you're a small fish in a big pond. Sometimes you have to settle for a small role. According to Ms. Young, you should feel lucky to get in at all. And getting a small part certainly doesn't justify destroying a library book. Tomorrow I expect you to go to the library and pay for the book with your own money."

"Fine! But you can't make me be in the play."

"Okay," he said. "One last thing. I was thinking that maybe I've been putting too much pressure on you, expecting too much from you. I'm going to ask Mrs. Whitehead to come over after school for the next few weeks and help, just until my work eases."

I groaned. "We don't want anybody else in the house."

"I think we need help. I think—"

I opened the door. "We don't need help! I'm not doing the play anyway."

Nutter came running down the hall and threw himself at Dad. "I'm sorry I ate the cake. Frankie shouldn't get into trouble for that. She takes good care of me. Don't ask Mrs. Whitehead. She has hairs coming out of her nose."

Dad cracked up.

Skip slithered into the hall. "It's true. We hate Mrs. Whitehead."

"All right." Dad gave in. "I won't ask Mrs. Whitehead to come, but you guys have to each promise something. Nutter, you have to promise not to eat cake before dinner. . . ."

Nutter saluted like a soldier.

"Skip, you have to mind your own business. It's okay to *play* at being a spy, but you shouldn't *really* spy on people."

Skip nodded, like *that* was going to stop him.
Dad turned to me.

"I know. I know," I said. "I have to pay for the library book."

"And . . ."

"And watch Nutter more closely after school."

"And help me with my koala costume!" Nutter exclaimed.

Dad ruffled Nutter's hair.

The phone rang, and Dad went to get it.

I grabbed Skip by his skinny little arm. "You dirty rotten pig. Spy on me e-mailing again, and I'll tell everybody in your class that you wet your bed."

"It's not true. I don't wet my bed."

I let go and crossed my arms. "I'm a very good actress, Skip. Even your friends will believe me."

That got him.

But I wasn't done. I needed more info. "How much of my e-mails to Ratlady did you read?" I asked.

"Nothing. I just saw her name. You deleted them faster than I could read them. Why are you writing to her anyway? Why is this such a big deal?"

"She's an enemy, Skip. She's trying to get her claws into Dad. You have to know who your enemies are." I slammed my door.

A minute later Dad knocked. "Hey, Frankie. Why is this door closed again? You can't stay angry."

"It's not because I'm angry," I lied. "I have a report to do. I work better in privacy."

"Well, come out anyway. It's Beth on the phone. She says she really wants to talk to you."

"I'm not in the mood for Beth," I said.

The last two things aren't lies. I'm not in the mood to talk to Beth, and I do have a report to do.

So am I writing my report? No, I am writing the saga of this evening. Although I'm feeling somewhat better now, I'm still mad at Skip. Perhaps I should sell him on eBay. I'm certainly never talking to him again. Now that Dad knows that I e-mailed Ratlady, he might find out what I've been e-mailing her about, and it will be all Skip's fault.

I'm starved, but I'm not coming out of this

room . . . at least not until Dad is working on his stupid dulcimer in the basement. Then I'm going to sneak out and go on-line. I have one absolutely last lie, which will absolutely convince Ratlady. Since Ratlady doesn't listen to me, I am going to write her a message and say it's from Dad. It's a dramatic, drastic idea, but these are dramatic, drastic times.

To: **Ayanna Bayo <ratlady@wz.org>**
From: **Robert Wallop <wallop@dman.com>**
Sent: **Tuesday, Oct. 21, 9:45 P.M.**
Subject: **Confession**

Dear Ayanna:
    This is Robert. I have something to confess. I will be getting married soon. I should have told you this right away. But I'm taking some medicine that confuses my mind. I hope that you will understand. It would be best for me and my family if you would stop communicating with me. If I call or write, it is because I am confused. Please ignore me.
    Thank you,
    Robert

To: **Robert Wallop <wallop@dman.com>**
From: **Ayanna Bayo <ratlady@wz.org>**
Received: **Tuesday, Oct. 21, 10:00 P.M.**
Subject: **Re: Confession**

Dear Frankie:

I can tell that you wrote the message. I am worried about you. Signing someone else's name to a message is serious. Here's what I think is happening: I think you feel threatened by the idea of your dad becoming romantically involved with me. You probably miss your mom a lot and worry about someone taking her place. This is understandable. It's called being "territorial."

Lots of animals are territorial for good reason: It helps them survive. Take naked mole-rats, for example. They live in very separate colonies, which are really big families. In the wild, if one mole-rat accidentally burrows into the tunnel system of another colony, the soldier mole-rats don't bother getting acquainted with the new mole-rat. They attack immediately. This behavior is ingrained in them. Biologists call it a survival instinct. The idea is that in order to survive, a colony must defend its

118

territory (that means its food supply) from others—even other mole-rats.

You're thinking of clever ways to try to dissuade me from having any further communication with your father. What you need to do is talk to him about all of this. Please, turn off the computer and tell your father how you feel.

Honestly and hopefully yours,
Ayanna

To: **Ayanna Bayo <ratlady@wz.org>**
From: **Robert Wallop <wallop@dman.com>**
Sent: **Tuesday, Oct. 21, 10:05 P.M.**
Subject: **FYI**

Dear Ms. Bayo:

I don't know what you're talking about. I didn't "sign" my dad's name to an e-mail message. I have been in my room writing in my diary.

I'll tell you one thing, though. It makes a lot of sense to me that one colony of naked mole-rats wouldn't want a rat from another colony barging in.

Frankie

Dear Frankie:

It does make a lot of sense for mole-rats to defend their colonies: An outsider threatens the food supply.

What about human relationships? New relationships do threaten to change old dynamics. But if we close ourselves to the possibility of new friendships, how do we ever grow?

I met your father because he came barging into the small mammal house to get out of the rain and accidentally bumped into me. If I immediately became angry and hostile toward him, then I wouldn't have gotten to know him. And that would have been a loss.

I have enjoyed getting to know him, hearing him talk about you and your brothers, and learning about dulcimers. A little over a week ago, I didn't know that the Wallop family or Pepper Blossom existed; now, I can picture you all in my mind. I didn't realize, until your dad barged in, just how boring my tunnel system had become.

Accidentally yours,

Ayanna

To: **Ayanna Bayo <ratlady@wz.org>**
From: **Robert Wallop <wallop@dman.com>**
Sent: **Tuesday, Oct. 21, 10:10 P.M.**
Subject: **Re: FYI**

Ms. Bayo:

I'm sorry for your boring life. My life is never boring. But if I were you, I wouldn't go falling in love with strangers. You never know about strangers. They might look nice on the outside and be nasty on the inside.

—F.

F.:
    You are absolutely right. It's wise to be cautious.
    —A.
P.S. I know that I promised not to tell your dad about our correspondence, but I'm not sure if I should keep that promise now. Your dad needs to know how you're feeling. I won't tell him, but only if you agree to talk to him.

    Fine.

Still Tuesday, 10:20 P.M.

Ratlady wants me to open up to Dad. How can I open up to someone who is keeping secrets from me?

I keep thinking about that letter that Dad wrote to her. *Your e-mails to Heartstrings haven't been distracting me from my work; they've been inspiring me.* What have they been writing to each other?

She agreed with me that it's wise to be cautious, but how far has her "friendship" with Dad gone?

I wish there would be a naked mole-rat emergency at her zoo that would take up all her attention. A hole in the plastic tunnel! Naked mole-rats escaping! If I lived in Washington, D.C., I'd sneak over to the zoo and create a diversion.

I'd like to talk to someone about all this, but who? I can't talk to Beth. She doesn't get it. I feel like I'm the last of my species alive on the face of the earth.

I'm crawling into bed. Good night.

Dear Diary,

I'm writing this in the girl's bathroom. That's the only place I can get a little privacy around here.

I can't believe how this day is going so far. It all started with math. I forgot we were having a test.

I have never been unprepared for a test in my life. Normally when I get a test, I know what to do and calmly do it. Today when Mr. Peter handed out the tests, I thought my eyeballs were going to explode. I stared at the first page, but I couldn't make sense of it. Meanwhile everybody around me started scribbling right away. I felt the way Helen Keller must have felt when she could feel people's lips moving but couldn't understand what they were saying. I felt like I was drowning.

Beth was already done with the first three problems. If I slumped in my seat and leaned a little to my left and squinted, I could see her answers floating on the page like life preservers.

In my moment of need, I did what I had never done before—I cheated. Halfway through, Beth glanced back at me a few times, as if she could feel my eyes grabbing on to her work.

At the end of the period, I was exhausted. It's very tiring to cheat. It takes a lot of concentration. Not only do you have to get the answers down right, but also you have to keep the guilt from melting your conscience into a puddle.

I fell asleep during science and woke up to the sound of Mrs. Keating yelling. I jumped up, sure she was yelling at me. But she was bawling out Johnny Nye for sneaking onto the Internet and playing a computer game when he was supposed to be doing research for the big report that's due on Friday.

While Mrs. Keating yelled at him, his eyes took on this familiar faraway look. Johnny has developed this way of disappearing inside himself, leaving only a blank look in his eyes and a half-smile on his lips that drive teachers crazy. His face has this movie-star handsome quality, except that he doesn't seem to be aware of it.

I don't know why Pepper Blossom hasn't shipped Johnny off to prison already. He gets into trouble every week. He got busted in kindergarten for stealing candy from Mae's, had to repeat second grade because he ditched school so often, and got suspended in the fourth grade for setting off a cherry bomb in the boys' bathroom. The thing about Johnny is that he knows a lot about some things—computers, for instance.

As Mrs. Keating yelled at him, it occurred to me that I was behaving just as badly. I wasn't doing my report either, but Mrs. Keating didn't suspect it. She assumed I was working because I'm Frankie Wallop. Straight-A student. So what was happening to me? Was I turning into a criminal?

Johnny must have felt me staring at him because he looked up and smiled. A thought crossed my mind, a bad thought, a criminal thought: I could ask Johnny Nye how to hack into Dad's business e-mail so that I could read any messages to and from Ratlady. Of all people, Johnny Nye would know how to do it.

The thought—or maybe the way Johnny was smiling at me—made me blush. Quickly I glanced at Beth, who was busy sharpening a colored pencil. From the looks of it, she was already finished with the report and was adding colorful accents to the cover. Goody-Goody Girl in action.

Should I ask Johnny Nye for help after school? Would he give it? It wouldn't be right to read Dad's business e-mail. But I deserved to know what was happening, didn't I?

During lunch, I decided to ask Goody-Goody Girl for a favor.

"Let me guess," she said. "You want to copy my science report or cheat on another test?" She raised her eyebrows.

I gave her my old Frankie smile. "I wasn't cheating, Beth. I was just checking to see if we had the same answers."

She shrugged.

"Come on, Beth. I really need a favor."

"Why should I do a favor for you? I've called you *three* times in the past four days, and you haven't wanted to talk."

How could I explain that I didn't want to talk to her because she doesn't understand what I'm going through? "I'm sorry," I said quickly. "I've been really crabby lately."

"No kidding."

"This thing with my dad and that Ratlady is driving me nuts."

She perked up at the topic. "Are they falling in love?"

I wanted to scream. The way she said it really bothered me. But I needed her help, so I said that I wanted to go to Heartstrings after school to talk to my dad about it without Skip and Nutter around. "Will you pick up Nutter and bring him to my house and baby-sit him just until I get home?" Beth can't resist Nutter. She's an only child.

"Well, stage crew isn't meeting today, so I guess I could," she said. "If you promise to tell me *everything*."

I agreed. Lie number one hundred and three.

Maybe I'll chicken out by the time school is over.

Isn't it strange that when you wake up in the morning you have no idea what will happen during the day? When I woke up this morning, I had no idea that the day would be a whirlwind of crime, unexpected encounters, and mind-blowing relevations (revealations? revelations?).

All afternoon I wondered if I'd have the guts to ask for Johnny's help to read Dad's business e-mail. At three o'clock I reminded Beth to pick up Nutter, and I left school, still wondering.

Johnny lives with his grandma in a trailer about a mile behind the town on Old School Road. He could ride the bus, but he always walks. I cut across the field, hoping no one would guess where I was going. Luckily Old School Road is pretty deserted. So once I got onto it, I was alone. Just as I came around the curve, I caught sight of him.

"Johnny," I called out.

He turned around and stared.

I wanted to run the other way, but I forced myself to keep walking until I caught up with him. "Hey," I said. "I was wondering if you could help me with something."

He didn't say a word. He just stared at me like he couldn't believe I was there. I couldn't believe it, either. I almost panicked, and then I remembered this acting technique where you "mirror" the person standing in front of you. I mirrored Johnny—slouching a little and letting my face take on this "I don't care" look, which made me relax and feel more confident. "I was wondering if you could teach me how to hack into my dad's business e-mail so that I can read his messages."

He laughed.

I guess he didn't expect that.

I waited a few seconds for him to say something. Anything. Desperately, I pulled out the wad of bills in my pocket (the money I had forgotten to give to the school librarian). "I can pay you."

Johnny nodded and took the bucks. "Come on."

He walked, and I followed. The sound of my shoes crunching on the gravel was embarrassingly loud, so I racked my brain for small talk to cover up the noise. "Mrs. Keating really got mad at you today."

Wow. What brilliant things would I think up next?

He kicked a stone. He shrugged. What else is new?

I confessed. "I was sleeping during class. I haven't even started the report."

He smiled. "Well, well, well. The perfect Frankie Wallop is going bad."

"I'm not going bad. I'm just . . ." I didn't know how to finish.

He kicked another stone. "So how come you want to snoop around in your dad's e-mail?"

"I . . ." I was hoping that a colorful lie would descend like a hot-air balloon from the heavens onto the gray and deserted road of my mind. Nothing came. The noise of my shoes on the gravel was ridiculous. I sounded like a circus elephant. He was looking at me. I had to say something. Why couldn't I think of what to say?

"It don't matter," he said, and shrugged. "None of my business."

We turned the corner, and there was the trailer parked in a clearing. Beyond it, the road kept stretching out in the loneliest way. It shouldn't be called Old School Road, it should be called Endangered Species Road, because nobody but Johnny lives on it.

We got to the trailer door and I froze. In the back of my mind I remembered the rumor about how Johnny was taken away from his mother and father when he was really little because they beat him and didn't feed him. Was I really going into Johnny Nye's trailer?

Just then a voice called out from behind the trailer, and an old woman walked out, ducking under T-shirts and towels hanging from a clothesline. Johnny's grandma. She doesn't go into town, so I don't know much about her except that her name is Elsie Nye and that she looks like a weed that the world has let grow wild. She has tangled gray hair that reaches all the way to her waist. Today she was wearing an old yellow dress over a pair of brown slacks. She had on work boots, like the kind my dad's friend Ozzie Filmore wears, and was carrying a bunch of vegetables in her arms.

There are two kinds of people in Pepper Blossom. There are folks like my dad, who weren't born here. They came here for college in Bloomington (which isn't far away) and loved it so much they stayed, either in Bloomington or in small towns like Pepper Blossom. Then there are the old-timers—people who've been living in these parts for generations. They live just outside of town, in trailers or old falling-down houses. They have their own way of being and their own country way of talking, using their own words for certain things. For example, instead of "grandma," it's "mammaw." Johnny's grandma is one of these people. So is Johnny.

"Hey, Mammaw," Johnny said. "This is Frankie Wallop. I'm helping her with something on the computer."

"Well that's sweet, Johnny." She was trying to carry too much, and an eggplant fell.

Johnny and I both bent to pick it up, and we almost bumped heads.

"Aren't they beauties?" she asked. "You like eggplant?"

I must have made a face because she laughed.

"How 'bout tomatoes? Everybody likes tomatoes. Ya'll grow any at your place?"

I shook my head.

She handed me a huge red tomato and said, "Well go over to the patch and help yourself. Thanks to this warm spell, they're still growing."

"We got to work on the computer, Mammaw," Johnny said, setting down a bucket for her to put the vegetables in. "Maybe you could pick her some."

I followed him up the steps to the trailer door, still holding that tomato like an idiot, not knowing what to do with it. Inside the trailer it was like a whole world crammed into a closet. On the right there was a small booth like in Mae's restaurant. There was a bright pink tablecloth on the table, but you could hardly see it because the table was full of cups and boxes and tools. Above it, a collection of chickens—chicken figurines and chicken salt-and-pepper shakers—was displayed on a shelf.

In the middle of the trailer were a tiny stove and refrigerator, stacked with pots and pans. Everything was very clean, and the whole place smelled like apple cider. It seemed old-fashioned—not like a place that would have a computer with Internet access.

On the left were two small beds, neatly made with crocheted blankets. One was topped with piles and piles of clothes. The other was topped with something I hadn't noticed right away—a very scratched-up old guitar.

"Is that yours?" I asked.

He picked it up. "I found it in the junkyard over at Gnawbone and fixed it up. Your dad helped me."

"Oh. Do you play?" Another brilliant question from yours truly.

He could have very easily made fun of me by saying, No, I just keep it around because we have so much room in here. But he didn't say anything. To my amazement he sat down on the bed and started to play. I didn't know what to do, so I just stood there and stared at the tomato I was still holding.

Slowly and steadily, he plucked out a song, a really pretty tune, like something you'd sing to a little kid who was scared. It filled the whole trailer. I could feel it coming up through the trailer floor and through the bottoms of my feet.

I said something really stupid, like "Wow," when he was done.

He looked at me, surprised.

I didn't know what to say next, so I said, "I can't stay very long because—"

"Right. The e-mail." He put down the guitar and pulled a laptop from under his bed. I wondered if he had stolen the computer, and then I felt guilty for wondering while he cleared a space on the table and plugged it into a phone jack.

There was only one place for me to sit: next to him in the booth. I set the tomato on a stack of plates and squeezed in.

I knew Dad's business e-mail address (DULCIMERMAN@DMAN.COM). And I guessed that he used the same password at work as he did at home. So it only took Johnny about two minutes to show me how to get in. It was easier than I thought.

Ayanna Bayo. Ayanna Bayo. Ayanna Bayo. There were about ten e-mails each day to and from Dad and Ratlady since Saturday. Ten e-mails each day!

"Dang. These guys like to write," Johnny said. "I don't have a printer, or I'd print them out for you."

"That's okay," I said, as he scrolled through.

"Where do you want to start? With today?"

I should have stopped right there and said thank you and walked away. But I nodded, and Johnny opened a message that Dad had sent about an hour before.

The words appeared on the screen in front of us. Johnny started reading out loud.

"How can a string of words reach you
    across the way?
Can this song find you and say all there is
    to say?

Letters of love, fragile and thin,
Sometimes get lost in the wind . . ."

He stopped. "It's a song," he said.

Listening to a boy read a love song written by your dad has to be one of the most embarrassing scenes in human history. It reminded me of the time Beth saw Dad in his underwear. Only this was five thousand times worse because this was Johnny Nye, not Beth.

"He sounds serious," Johnny said. "Who is she?"

"You can close it. I don't need to see any more." I got up so fast I pulled the tablecloth, and the dishes rattled. My face felt like a field that had caught fire. "Thanks a lot," I said quickly. "See you."

I walked out the door. To my dismay, Johnny followed. I didn't want to have to think of anything else to say. I just wanted to get out of there.

His grandma was talking to two chickens over by a little shed I hadn't noticed. She stood up and looked at me as if surprised. "Who's this, Johnny?"

Her question caught me off guard. My brain was already overloaded. How could she not remember me?

Johnny stepped in. "It's Frankie Wallop, Mammaw." His voice was patient and soft. "I was showing her something on the computer."

"It's nice to meet you, Frankie." She smiled, and the empty look in her eyes made me feel so sad, I had to look away. She really didn't remember meeting me. Was this Alzheimer's?

The whole picture: Johnny and his grandma on this lonely road with the trailer and the chickens . . . I was *seeing* it, but I couldn't imagine *living* it.

"I'm gonna walk Frankie home," Johnny said.

I didn't even have a chance to digest that statement because what he did next blew me away. Tough Johnny Nye, the kid who gets into trouble for ditching school and cussing teachers and setting off cherry bombs, walked over and gave his grandma a kiss on the cheek.

I didn't know what to say, so I just started walking.

"See if your girlfriend wants any tomatoes, Johnny," his grandma called.

I'm sure she meant girl friend and not *girlfriend,* but I was too embarrassed to look at Johnny. I kept walking. He caught up to me with two tomatoes in his hands and an embarrassed look on his face.

"Sorry about that girlfriend thing," he mumbled. "She didn't know what she was saying."

"That's okay," I said. I wanted to ask him about his grandma's memory and how bad it was and how long she'd been that way. And I wanted to tell him how sweet he was with her. But I kept my mouth shut.

We walked in silence. After a while he looked at me and said, "I thought that was pretty cool."

"What?"

"Your dad writing that song."

I was too shocked to say a word.

"I like writing songs," he said, and I wondered if he had written the song he had played. "How come you don't like her?" he asked.

"Ratlady? Because I don't want my dad to get involved with anybody."

"Where does she live?"

"Washington, D.C."

He whistled. We kept walking.

"How'd they meet?" he asked.

"At a conference."

"Love at first sight, huh?"

I shrugged.

"Do you believe in it?" he asked.

"In what?"

"Love at first sight."

A hot-air balloon from Mars could have landed in front of us and I wouldn't have been any more surprised than I was by the way this conversation was going. When I finally found my voice, I stammered, "I—I th-think that it's wise to be cautious. I think you have to get to know somebody first."

How stupid.

He didn't say anything, and we walked a ways without talking. Then he turned to me. His eyes were as blue as the sky, and he was smiling, as if he were telling himself a joke.

He held up a tomato. "You think it's like this?" he asked.

"What?"

"Maybe you think love is like a tomato. It has to grow."

On the outside I probably looked like a normal girl walking along a gravel road. But inside I was screaming: *Johnny Nye is talking to me about love being like tomatoes!* I was screaming at myself so loud that I forgot he had asked me a question.

"Sorry," he said. "I don't know why I asked you that. You're all red."

I looked at him. "Your face is red, too."

He smiled. "We're a couple of walking tomatoes."

We both laughed, and I felt myself turn even redder. I couldn't possibly think of what to say next, and I knew that he couldn't think of what to say, either. We just kept looking at those two big red tomatoes, and it was like he was holding our embarrassment in his hands.

And then Johnny did this funny thing. He stopped and threw one of the tomatoes at a tree. He just let it fly, and it hit the trunk with a satisfying *splat!*

"Your turn," he said, and handed me the other tomato.

I pitched it . . . *splat!*

He laughed. "Frankie Wallop, you got a pretty good arm."

"Thank you."

"Were you pretending to aim at that Rat-lady's face?"

I laughed.

Whatever felt awkward between the two of us had flown out and splattered like those tomatoes. We walked for a while and talked about teachers and school. I asked if he was going to the Fall Festival, and without thinking I blurted out, "You should sign up for the open mike."

He looked at me as if I'd just told him to go visit the president. "You mean you think I should play?"

"If you want to. I mean, anybody can sign up. You should sign up. If you want to."

He stuck his hands into his pockets. "I've seen you play with the Red Beet Ramblers, and I saw you in that school show last year. You're good."

I almost fell down dead. When I performed I didn't really think about who was in the audience, other than Dad and Grandma. It was unbelievably strange to think that Johnny Nye watched me sing onstage and had an opinion about me.

"I think I'd be too nervous to sing in front of lots of people," he said.

"It's not so bad once you get going."

"You made it for the play this semester, didn't you?"

"I made it. But I didn't get the part I wanted."

"Haxer's an idiot," he said.

I laughed, and he smiled.

"Who got the part you wanted?"

I rolled my eyes. "Melinda Bixby."

"Bixby? Next to you, she's a cow!"

We both laughed.

We got to my street, and I stopped. The last thing I needed was to be seen with Johnny Nye. My reputation was in trouble right now.

If I were seen with Johnny, it would go right down the drain.

"Well, thanks again," I said.

A look came into his eyes like he could read my mind. He reached into his pocket and took out the money. He gave it back, his fingers brushing my hand.

"But—"

"I don't want it," he said. "I'll help you for nothing. If you want, I can . . ."

Did he want to get together again? Was he offering more help? Did he like me? It was all too confusing. I said good-bye and hurried home.

I was dying to shut myself in my room and write about everything that had happened.

Unfortunately, I didn't have time because Beth pounced on me the minute I walked through the door. "Come and listen to this. It is so amazing." She pulled me into the dining room. Skip and Nutter were sitting at the table with Skip's spy recorder.

Skip grinned at me. "We were playing outside, and I overheard Mrs. Holmes talking on the phone on her back patio, so I taped her. Listen. . . ."

I looked at Beth. "I'm not talking to Skip, Beth. He is a traitor as well as a spy."

"You're going to want to hear this, Frankie," he said while he rewound the tape.

"I don't want to hear it again," Nutter complained. "I want you guys to help me make my koala costume."

"I don't want to hear it, either," I said. "You promised you were going to stop spying on people."

"You've got to hear it," Beth said. "We've already listened to it three times."

Skip pushed the button, and Mrs. Holmes's voice started in midsentence: ". . . is falling apart. . . . I agree. . . . Yes, and I heard that Robert is having a nervous breakdown. . . . It's true. . . . Well, yes. . . . I think there's only one thing that would truly help. We need to fix him up with somebody, Susan. They need a woman in that house, don't you know it?"

"Oh great!" I exclaimed. "Now Mrs. Holmes is going to try to fix Dad up with somebody."

"What does 'fix up' mean?" Nutter asked. "I don't get it."

Beth explained, "It means finding him a girlfriend to marry."

Nutter's eyes grew large. "Dads can't have girlfriends, can they?"

Skip looked suitably horrified. Maybe now he would understand what I meant by knowing our enemies.

"We do *not* need a woman in the house," I said. "If everybody would just leave us alone—"

"Shhh!" Beth said. "Listen to what comes next."

Mrs. Holmes's voice continued on tape: ". . . Yes, I do have someone in mind. . . ."

I stared at Beth. Her eyes were wide and crazy-looking, like she didn't know whether to laugh or scream.

"Who?" I asked.

"Shhh! It's coming. . . ."

"I think the perfect match," Mrs. Holmes said, "would be Doris Trolly."

I could have dropped dead.

Mrs. Holmes rambled on. "She's single. She

can cook for an army. Did you taste her lasagna at the potluck? And she's a guidance counselor, Susan. Why, she could help him with his problems. And I think she's as cute as a button, in her way."

Beth laughed.

"It's not funny, Beth!"

"I'm not laughing at the situation," Beth said. "I'm laughing because she said 'cute as a button.'"

"What does she look like?" Nutter asked.

"Like a troll," Beth said.

"Or an army tank with fangs," I said, and Beth laughed again.

Skip turned off his recorder, grinning with spy satisfaction. I could tell he thought that he had made up for spying on me last night.

I groaned.

"What are you going to do?" Beth asked.

"I'll keep spying on Mrs. Holmes," Skip announced. "Agent Skip Wallop on active duty!"

"Can I help?" Nutter asked.

The two of them ran off to assemble spy gear.

"I wouldn't worry about it," Beth said. "I doubt The Troll is looking for love. She probably doesn't even know what love is."

Beth was staring at me, waiting for me to agree. I didn't know what to think about The Troll. I couldn't concentrate. I kept thinking about the whole scene with Johnny Nye and about the love song my dad had written to Ratlady.

As nonshalantly (nonchalantly?) as possible, I got rid of Beth and came up here to write. Now my hand is killing me. I probably have carple (carpul? carpel?) tunnel syndrome.

As I said, it has been a whirlwind of a day.

8:45 P.M.

The whirlwind continues! Things got worse after Beth left. Dad came home from work at 6:20 P.M. and had a fit because the house was a mess. At breakfast he had made us promise to clean the house after school because the Fall Festival music committee was meeting here at 6:30.

I had forgotten all about it. Every time I looked at him, I just kept thinking about all those e-mails at his shop. My boring, bushy-bearded father was carrying on a secret life. How could I possibly trust him about anything?

We finished stuffing all our junk into the closet as the doorbell rang.

"Get it, will you, Frankie?" Dad called from the kitchen. "I'm making coffee."

I opened the door. Standing there like an overgrown trick-or-treater was none other than The Troll. Ms. Doris Trolly. I almost screamed. She was wearing a green velvet jogging suit and lipstick. Pink!

"Hello, Francine," she said. "May I come in?"

She introduced herself to Dad, and I was waiting for her to mention the forged note about the fake dentist's appointment. But she handed him a plate of cheese and crackers and explained that Mrs. Holmes suggested she join the Fall Festival music committee since she had an interest in music.

"What kind of music?" asked Dad.

"All kinds!" she said, obviously lying through her fangs.

"Wonderful!" Dad said. "We're happy to have you." He set the cheese and crackers on the coffee table.

My face turned green.

The Troll glanced at the red chair hanging from the ceiling and said, "What a fascinating decorating idea." What she meant was, "I wouldn't put that in my house if you paid me."

The others arrived, and Skip and Nutter and I spied on them from the kitchen. The Troll practically knocked over Nelson Wicks to get the chair next to Dad's. All through the meeting she kept laughing and placing her hand on Dad's arm. The Troll, the guidance counselor, was *flirting* with my dad. She wasn't looking for love. She was grabbing it by the throat.

The meeting was over in an hour, but she insisted on staying to help wash the cups and plates. Skip, Nutter, and I ran down the stairs to the basement to continue our spying from there.

On Dad's workbench the dulcimer he was making was all laid out, and I was shocked to see how far he'd gotten. He must have worked on it all night. Dad usually makes his dulcimers from blond wood and carves flowers and diamonds and hearts into them. The one he made for my mom, which is now mine, has a vine with tiny heart-shaped flowers made of pearl. This one is a deep brown. Carved into the fingerboard is a parade of animals—a tiny giraffe, a lion, an elephant, and a zebra.

It was the most beautiful one I had ever seen, and it made me angry to think that he was making it for this woman that he just met. I imagined what I would feel like if I opened a box and saw this. Ratlady will go crazy over it. She'll hop on the next plane heading west. She won't care where it stops; she'll parachute out over Pepper Blossom.

I ran my finger along the fingerboard, feeling the carved animals like Braille. I imagined smashing it into pieces, stuffing it into the fireplace, and lighting a match. But I couldn't give it a single scratch. There were four silver tuning pegs lying next to the dulcimer. I slipped them into my pocket. Dad had more supplies at Heartstrings, but if I took these I might slow him down a little.

Skip motioned to Nutter and me and whispered, "We can hear what they're saying through here." He pointed to the heating vent.

I squatted down with Skip and Nutter.

We could hear kitchen sounds, then The Troll's muffled voice, "What an interesting idea for wallpaper!"

She was probably staring in horror at all the postcards that Mom had put up.

"My wife had a wonderful sense of play," Dad said.

"It must be difficult managing a household on your own."

"I'm doing all right."

The water turned on.

"Do you enjoy cooking, Robert?"

"I enjoy eating." Dad laughed.

Skip whispered, "My spying skills are really paying off. Aren't they, Frankie?"

"Shhh!" I said.

"I love to cook!" The Troll continued.

"Lasagna is my specialty. But it's silly to cook a whole lasagna for one person." She waited, but Dad didn't say anything. "I know!" she exclaimed. "I'll make a lasagna and bring you over some."

Skip and I looked at each other.

Nutter whispered, "I don't like lasagna, do I, Frankie?"

I shook my head, waiting and hoping to hear Dad say no thanks.

"That's very thoughtful of you, Doris. But we're doing fine."

Miracle of miracles! Good going, Dad!

She went on. "I didn't want to mention anything in front of the others, but I have to tell you that I'm worried about Francine."

"Frankie?"

"She has been showing signs of . . . well, stress, perhaps. I don't know Francine. But from what I've heard, she's never had any problems with behavior . . . until now."

Dad was silent.

"Mr. Haxer is worried about her and—"

"We've talked about the play—"

"And her other teachers have noticed that

she seems to be having trouble focusing. Mr. Peter is concerned that she may have cheated on a math test today. . . ."

Skip's mouth dropped open. Listening to Trolly fire off a list of my sins was the thrill of his young life.

"The librarian said that she hasn't returned a book that Mr. Haxer really needs. Her science teacher is worried that she hasn't produced a rough draft of her report."

The perfect, smooth, straight-A exterior was starting to crumble. I held my breath, waiting for the bomb about the dentist to drop. But Dad jumped in.

"Thank you for your concern, Doris. I appreciate it. It was a real blow for Frankie not to get a lead in the play. But that's all there is to it. I'll talk to her about it—"

"That's the right instinct, Robert."

"I've been on her case lately. Maybe I've been putting too much pressure on her. She takes care of Skip and Nutter after school. I've been wondering if I should get some help. If she isn't getting her homework done, maybe she needs more guidance after school."

At the word *guidance* it sounded like The Troll was starting to pant. "I could pop over after school a few times a week if you like."

Skip pretended to vomit, and Nutter started cracking up.

"Shhh!" I whispered.

"Really," she continued. "It wouldn't be a problem at all. I'm single, you know. I don't have many responsibilities, other than my work right now." The Troll rolled on. "Junior high school is a big transition, Robert. Some kids lose their way and get in with the wrong crowd. You really have to stay on top of it. You know, I saw Francine walking after school with Johnny Nye. He is a terrible influence, from what I've heard."

"Really?"

"You've got to watch your own health, too. I'm sure it's very stressful being a single father. It isn't a bad thing to admit that you might need a little help. If you'd like, I'll keep a closer eye on Francine at school and schedule some regular counseling appointments with her."

She wants to be my Miracle Worker; she wants to save me from myself.

Dad chirped, "That would be great, Doris."

"And if you ever need anyone to talk to . . ." Her voice was as pink and slippery as her awful lipstick.

"Thanks . . . and thanks for the help tonight. Let me walk you out."

They moved out of the kitchen, so we couldn't hear any more.

"Come on," Skip whispered. "We have to sneak upstairs so Dad doesn't know we were spying." We ran into my room. Nutter and Skip sat on my bed and pretended to be reading, and I sat at my desk and pretended to work on my report. Dad came up a minute later.

"Wow, look at you guys, reading and doing homework," he said. "Quiet as mice the whole time."

Skip gave me a secret glance of triumph. Then Nutter blurted out, "Don't let the army tank come over. I don't like lasagna."

Dad looked at all three of us and burst out laughing. "That's why you were so quiet. You were spying."

Skip socked Nutter in the arm. "You had to tell!"

"Army tank?" Dad asked. "Who came up with that?"

Nutter pointed at me.

"Well, she has a good heart," he said. "I suppose you heard that she's concerned about your behavior, Frankie. We need to talk—"

Nutter stood up. "Talk. Talk. You always need to talk to Frankie, Dad. You're gonna talk her face right off her head."

Dad laughed again and scooped up Nutter. "All right, little Nutter Butter. No talking now. I'm taking you to bed."

"I want Frankie to help me with my costume," he protested.

"Tomorrow," Dad promised. As he carried Nutter out the door, he turned and gave me this look that said he'd be back.

While he read to Nutter, I thought about how awful it would be to have regular counseling sessions with Trolly. She didn't care about me. She wanted to "help" me in order to get in good with Dad.

Ten or fifteen minutes later, he came in. "Glad to see you didn't lock me out," he said with a smile.

Very funny.

"Frankie, I don't want to 'talk your face off' like Nutter said. But Ms. Trolly brought up a few things we should clear up."

I thought about suggesting that we clear up some of his little issues, such as ditching meetings and sending secret e-mails and taking secret phone calls and making secret dulcimers, but I realized that I needed to focus on getting myself out of trouble. My brain was going a mile a minute.

"About the cheating . . . ," he said.

I fingered the tuning pegs in my pocket. I could lie and deal with my own guilt or I could confess and deal with Dad's anger and disappointment. I crossed my arms and looked indignant. "I did *not* cheat. Mr. Peter has no proof. I was just looking up from my paper now and then to give my eyes a rest. My eyes have been hurting lately. You can either believe me or not."

"Fine. I believe you, Frankie. I know you're not a cheater."

I took a breath. That wasn't so bad. The old straight-A, choir-singing reputation comes through again.

"Now, about the library book?"

I jumped in. Better to get this over quickly. "I brought the money in, but I was so busy I didn't get the chance to go to the library. I'll do it first thing in the morning."

"Promise?"

"Promise."

That wasn't so bad, either.

He sat on my bed and rubbed his beard. The science report was coming next, "So what about this science report? I haven't heard a word about it, and Ms. Trolly said it's due Friday. You have to be using reference materials, illustrations, and everything."

"No problem," I said. "I'm almost done."

"Really? What's it about?"

I panicked, looking around for an idea; and then I saw the naked mole-rat book Skip had left on my bed.

"It's about naked mole-rats," I said.

Dad grinned, of course. "Really? That's interesting."

"See?" I handed him the book. "I'm using this."

"I'll have to tell that woman I met at the zoo."

He was such a liar. He couldn't even say her name out loud.

"Can I see your rough draft?"

I shuffled some papers. "Well, I haven't written it out yet. But I know a lot. That's why I was e-mailing her, you know, to get more information. I know how mole-rats work cooperatively to survive, how they live in tunnels in parts of Africa where the soil is very hard and dry, how they form an assembly line to dig, how they eat sweet potatoes and other root vegetables, how they each have different tasks, how the queen is in charge, and how the soldiers defend their territory from predators and even naked mole-rats from other colonies."

"Wow!" he said. "That's amazing."

It was amazing. I really didn't know that I knew so much.

"Sounds like all you need to do is write it down. You've got to come home after school tomorrow and just do it, okay?"

I nodded.

"Do I need to ask Mrs. Whitehead to come over to help with Skip and Nutter so you can concentrate?"

"No."

"Okay. Now I want to talk about Johnny Nye."

I turned as red as one of Elsie Nye's tomatoes and protested that there was nothing going on.

"I didn't think anything was going on," he said, and I turned redder. "I just wanted you to know, Frankie, that I didn't like the way Ms. Trolly talked about Johnny. She's assuming he's bad to the core. Johnny's had some tough breaks, and he has made some mistakes, but he's got a lot more going for him than people in this town realize. He essentially takes care of both himself and his grandma. He's a smart kid, although I bet his report card doesn't show it."

I pictured Johnny fixing up an old guitar, Johnny pulling out that computer and hooking it up, Johnny figuring it all out on his own.

Dad continued. "You know his grand-mother doesn't even know how to read?"

I shook my head, but I wasn't surprised. Did he know that she couldn't remember things? I wondered.

"Anyway, I think it's fine if you're nice to Johnny," he continued. "He could use a friend. Just use good judgment and don't get into trouble."

"He's not my boyfriend or anything."

"Okay."

"We just happened to be walking down the street at the same time. I came home right after school. You can ask Skip." (I had paid Skip another dollar to keep the secret about Beth baby-sitting.)

"That's fine, Frankie." He patted me on the knee. "Why don't you spend a little more time on that report and then get to bed?"

Things aren't turning out so bad. The thing about Dad is that he wants to believe that everything is okay. The report on naked mole-rats was a brilliant idea. He really be-lieves that I was just getting information about them from Ratlady. If she doesn't say more to him, then I won't get into trouble.

As for the romance between Ratlady and Dad . . . At least I can keep track of it by logging on to Dad's office e-mail. Johnny showed me how to do it from home. Tomorrow after school I'll check all the messages.

I just need to finish that stupid report. I am going to do it right now.

10:00 P.M.

I actually wrote a stunning first paragraph for my science report, and then the most amazing thing happened. The doorbell rang at about 9:30 P.M. I thought it was The Troll, back to flirt some more, so I snuck to the top of the stairs where I could see the front door.

Dad opened it, and guess who was standing there in the glow of the porch light?

Johnny Nye.

"Hey, Johnny," Dad said. "What are you doing here?"

Over Dad's shoulder, Johnny caught sight of me standing there like an idiot in my pajamas. He smiled, and I ducked back.

"My grandma wanted ya'll to have these." He held out a paper bag.

Dad looked inside. "Tomatoes?"

I thought I was going to faint.

"We got too many to use," Johnny said. "And she thought you'd like them."

Dad laughed. "It seems everybody in Pepper Blossom wants to bring us food!" I could tell by his voice that he thought it was a strange coincidence for Johnny to drop by at 9:30 P.M. with tomatoes on the same night we were talking about him.

I was worried that Dad was going to say something about that or that Johnny was going to say something about how I'd been over at the trailer. But Johnny said good-bye and turned around to leave.

"Wait," Dad said. "How's the guitar going?"

"Been playing so much I got calluses." Johnny held out his left hand. "Check it out."

Dad looked at Johnny's fingers. "That's good! I bet it doesn't hurt to play now."

Johnny nodded. The next part came out hesitantly, like he wasn't sure if he really wanted to be saying what he was saying. "I've been thinking about maybe signing up for the open mike at the Fall Festival."

"That's a great idea, Johnny. All you've got to do is show up with your guitar and sign up."

Johnny nodded, still considering.

"Ever play in front of anybody before?" Dad asked.

Johnny glanced up at me. "Sort of," he said.

"Well I'd love to see your name on the list, Johnny."

Johnny nodded again.

"Hey, you want to see the new dulcimer I'm working on? I'm really excited about it."

"Sure."

I couldn't believe what I was hearing. My own dad doesn't tell me anything, and he goes and shows the secret dulcimer off to Johnny Nye.

They left. I didn't know what to do. I kept staring at the paper bag full of tomatoes sitting by the front door, thinking about everything that had happened today.

They came back up after about fifteen minutes, laughing and talking.

"See you, Mr. Wallop. Hope you find those tuning pegs."

"See you, Johnny. Tell your grandma thanks."

Before he left, Johnny glanced up one more time. I waved and smiled stupidly and ducked back again before Dad could see me.

Johnny's grandma didn't send him over to deliver tomatoes. She probably doesn't even remember that I was at the trailer today. So why did Johnny come? Did he come to ask my dad about the open mike? Or did he come for another reason?

How am I possibly going to fall asleep tonight?

Good morning, Frankie:

Your dad called late last night. He told me the story about Skip spying on you and how you admitted that you had been e-mailing me with questions about naked mole-rats. Even though you just said it was about naked mole-rats, I think that's a good start. He also said that you're doing a report on naked mole-rats. Is that true? If so, how fun. Let me know if you have any questions. I'd love to see the report when you're done.

Yours truly,

Ayanna

To: **Ayanna Bayo <ratlady@wz.org>**
From: **Robert Wallop <wallop@dman.com>**
Sent: **Thursday, Oct. 23, 7:15 A.M.**
Subject: **Re: To Frankie**

Dear Ms. Bayo:

Skip does all sorts of bad things and never gets into any trouble. I wish my dad would send him off to a military boarding school congested with rats in Texas.

I have so much to do today. Just thinking about it makes me want to explode. How am I supposed to go to school, come home, write a report (yes, it's true), do all the rest of my homework, and make a koala costume for Nutter when there is so much on my mind? So much is happening to me that I don't even feel like me.

Frankie

To: Robert Wallop <wallop@dman.com>
From: Ayanna Bayo <ratlady@wz.org>
Received: Thursday, Oct. 23, 7:33 A.M.
Subject: Re: To Frankie

Dear Frankie:

What an honest e-mail. I can really hear your frustration. Is there someone at school with whom you can share your feelings and concerns? A teacher or a guidance counselor?

Yours truly,

Ayanna

To: Ayanna Bayo <ratlady@wz.org>
From: Robert Wallop <wallop@dman.com>
Sent: Thursday, Oct. 23, 7:35 A.M.
Subject: Re: To Frankie

Dear Ms. Bayo:

Ha! You have no idea how funny that is. The teachers in junior high school are not like the teachers in elementary school. They are machines, not people. The guidance counselor's name is Doris Trolly, and she has the hots for my dad. She'd love it if I spilled my guts to her. Believe it or not, she came over last night, which was like a surprise blind date for my dad that our nosy neighbor, Mrs. Holmes, set up. She wants to make us her famous lasagna. It probably tastes like the muck that's under Dead Man's Creek.

Disgustedly yours,

Frankie

P.S. Gotta go. If I'm late for school, I'll probably be expelled.

Thursday, October 23, 12:20 P.M.

Dear Diary:

I'm in the nurse's office again with another headache.

The nurse almost didn't let me stay. "Another headache, Frankie?" she asked when I first walked in. "Maybe you should talk about these 'headaches' with Ms. Trolly instead of coming here."

At the mention of The Troll's name, I must have turned green, because the nurse let me lie down. Why does everyone in the world want me to talk about my problems with The Troll?

Today is the worst day of my life. Upon arrival at school, Beth grabbed me and pulled me into the girls' bathroom.

The whole next scene seemed to happen in slow motion.

"Everybody knows!" she whispered, her face full of panic.

"Knows what?"

"Knows about you and Johnny Nye! Frankie, it's not true, is it?"

Melinda and Denise walked in. "Hey, it's Johnny Nye's girlfriend," Melinda said, and Denise giggled. "What did you do with him after school yesterday, Frankie?"

I stood in the bathroom, listening to her words bounce off the walls. How did everybody find out? The Troll told Dad that she had seen us. Did she spread the rumor? I could see myself in the mirror. I looked very calm on the outside; but I was experiencing a major interior earthquake. The techtonic (techtonik? tectonic?) plates of my soul were pulling apart. Everything was buckling and shifting and cracking up inside me. I put a hand on the sink to steady myself.

The door opened. Who next? I thought. The Troll rolled in. "Girls, the bell has rung. Get to class *now*."

Beth ran out. Melinda and Denise followed.

"Oh, good morning, Francine," The Troll said when she saw that it was me still standing at the sink.

If it had been anybody else, I would have dropped to the floor and curled up in a ball and refused to come out. But I couldn't fall apart in front of The Troll; it would only give her more excuses to talk to Dad.

I grabbed my backpack and walked to class without looking at anybody. I could feel Beth's eyes on me as I passed her desk, and I could sense Johnny slumped in the back.

I got out my book, feeling the eyes of everybody drilling into me. People were whispering and laughing. I opened my book and stared at the numbers.

During Mr. Peter's lesson Jerry Parks tapped me on the shoulder. A moment later a note landed on my desk. "It's from Johnny," Jerry whispered.

I stared at the note. How could Johnny pass me a note? Didn't he know that passing me a note would make it worse? I tried to cover it with my hand before anybody noticed.

"Frankie," Mr. Peter's voice boomed. "Bring that up here."

If you get caught passing a note in Mr. Peter's class, you have to read it out loud, which is why nobody passes notes in his class.

"I didn't write it," I protested.

"I don't care. I saw it on your desk."

He leaned against his desk and crossed his arms, waiting.

I opened it.

Dear Frankie:
    I love you. I want to kiss you. Will you meet me after school in my trailer?
    Your boyfriend,
    Johnny

I couldn't possibly read it out loud. Reading it out loud would mean instant death. I wanted to glare at Johnny, to burn a hole through his skull with my eyes; but if I did, everybody would know that the note was from him. I've never hated anybody so much in my life. How could he do this to me?

Mr. Peter took the note from me and read it silently, his battery-operated face turning into a surprised human face.

Please don't say anything. Please don't say anything.

He handed the note back to me and looked at Johnny. "Mr. Nye, you can spend the rest of the period talking to Ms. Trolly."

The class went crazy.

Johnny exploded. "What did I do?"

Jerry Parks whispered something to Johnny, and Johnny shoved Jerry out of his desk. "That's enough!" Mr. Peter shouted. "Get out, Johnny."

Johnny stormed out of the room.

Jerry poked me and whispered, "Now your boyfriend is in trouble."

All morning the teasing continued like a steady rain.

At lunch I tried to talk to Beth, but we ended up getting into a big fight.

"Frankie, I heard you went to his trailer after school yesterday and kissed him," she whispered.

"That isn't true! I did go to his trailer. But we didn't do anything. He was teaching me something on the computer."

"You lied to me, Frankie. You told me you were going to Heartstrings, and you hung out with Johnny Nye? I wouldn't go to Johnny Nye's trailer if you paid me."

"You don't understand, Beth."

"No, *you* don't understand, Frankie. Your whole reputation is going down the drain. You ditched school. You forged a note. You lied to me. If you hang out with Johnny Nye, nobody is going to want to hang out with you. I'm telling you this because you're my friend."

"Some friend," I said.

She looked like she was going to cry. I should have said something, but she picked up her tray and walked away.

I didn't know what to do. I pretended that I didn't mind sitting all by myself in the cafeteria. I pretended that I really wanted to eat my apple. And then I threw away my lunch and walked to the nurse's office.

The nurse has just gone to the teachers' lounge to heat up her lunch, which is why I'm able to write.

12:40 P.M.

As Ms. Young always used to say, wonders never cease. A minute ago the back door to the nurse's office opened, the one that opens into the dead-end hallway by the art room, and Johnny slipped in.

I almost threw my notebook at him. "Leave me alone," I whispered. "I hate you. If you ever write me another note, I'll—"

He was looking at me, his eyes burning up whatever I was going to say. Then he gave me something and slipped out the door.

It all happened in a few seconds, and I was

staring at a note that had landed in my hands like a wild bird.

Dear Frankie:

I didn't write that note. Jerry wrote it and signed my name. I'd never do anything to get you into trouble.

Trolly told me to stay away from you. She said that kids like me are poison. She's probably right. I'm not like the guys who are in the school plays and on student council.

I'm sorry this is happening. You probably hate me and don't want to see me again. I won't talk to you, if that's what you want. I'll pretend that I hate you, if you want me to.

But yesterday was the best day of my life. If I were Mr. Haxer, I'd give every part in every play to you. If I were Mr. Peter, I'd never give you any homework. If I were a farmer, I'd give away ten thousand tons of tomatoes just to see you smile.

Johnny

Dear Ayanna:

You're right. Letters should be private. And I think it's wrong for somebody to write a fake letter and sign someone else's name to it.

There's a boy at school named Johnny Nye who likes me. Somebody wrote a nasty letter to me and signed his name. For a while I believed it.

Everybody thinks he's a no-good troublemaker, but they don't see the real Johnny Nye. He wrote me a real letter today. I've never received anything like it before. It was like a poem. I imagined what it would feel like if somebody at school got hold of it and read it, and the thought of that makes me sick.

Johnny showed me how to hack into my dad's business e-mail so that I could read your messages. (It was my idea, not his.) I was going to do it after school today, but now I'm not. It just doesn't seem right.

I don't know what to do about Johnny. He says

that he'll pretend to hate me, if that's what I want, to keep people from talking. That would be the easiest. Things could go back to normal. But there are two problems: The first is that I don't know what normal is for me anymore. The second is that I don't hate him. Johnny is about the only person I know right now who seems real. All the other kids at school are like robots; they behave a certain way because they're supposed to. They make automatic decisions about other people without even bothering to get to know them. They tease other people without even bothering to wonder how it feels.

Sadly yours,
Frankie

To: **Robert Wallop <wallop@dman.com>**
From: **Ayanna Bayo <ratlady@wz.org>**
Received: **Thursday, Oct. 23, 4:10 P.M.**
Subject: **Re: Stuff**

Dear Frankie:

I'm glad I checked my e-mail. Sounds like you had a very rough day. School can be a difficult place, and kids can be cruel to each other. There's an old African proverb: Before you poke a baby bird with a pointed stick, you should try it on yourself first to feel how it hurts. The world would be a better place if everybody remembered that.

You said it would be easier if you and Johnny pretended to hate each other. I'm not so sure about that. Lies are hard to keep up. They have a way of backfiring, or of eating you from the inside out.

Be true to your heart, Frankie. In the long run, it's much easier.

Love,

Ayanna

P.S. I'm glad that you realized the importance of privacy, although it sounds like you learned the lesson the hard way. If you have any questions about my relationship with your dad, you should ask your dad directly. The two of you really need to talk about all this. Have I said that enough?

To: Ayanna Bayo <ratlady@wz.org>
From: Robert Wallop <wallop@dman.com>
Sent: Thursday, Oct. 23, 4:15 P.M.
Subject: Re: Stuff

Dear Ayanna:

It sounds easy to be true to your heart, but you don't live in Pepper Blossom. Sometimes I hate this place. Everybody sticks their noses into everybody's business. There's no room to just *be*. I feel like I'm stuck in a tunnel, and I can't get out.

    —F.

To: Robert Wallop <wallop@dman.com>
From: Ayanna Bayo <ratlady@wz.org>
Received: Thursday, Oct. 23, 4:17 P.M.
Subject: Re: Stuff

Dear Frankie:

What you said about being stuck in a tunnel reminds me of something. Once when I was doing research on naked mole-rats in graduate school, I saw the queen of a colony pick on one mole-rat and shove her around a lot more than the others. I never figured out why the queen singled her out. After being repeatedly shoved and pushed by the queen, this female began to withdraw from the colony's activity. Then, a few other mole-rats in the colony began to follow the queen's example and treat the mole-rat roughly. Pretty soon all the mole-rats in the colony were "going along with the crowd" and persecuting her. After a while, the poor female sat by herself in the toilet chamber. She stopped eating and didn't go back to the nest to sleep. Eventually, she died. It was the saddest thing. I wanted that little naked mole-rat to stand up for herself, or to dig a new tunnel and establish a new home. But it doesn't work that way among mole-rats. Naked mole-rats can't exist by themselves.

—A.

To: Ayanna Bayo <ratlady@wz.org>
From: Robert Wallop <wallop@dman.com>
Sent: Thursday, Oct. 23, 4:19 P.M.
Subject: Re: Stuff

Dear Ayanna:

The kids at my school *are* naked mole-rats. They were bad enough when it was just a rumor about Johnny and me. I can't imagine how they'd act if we started openly hanging out together.

I can't possibly go to school tomorrow or next week.

I wish I could catch a disease so that I could spend a month in a hospital, watch TV all day, and have my food brought to me on trays. I wish I had a little gardener's cottage like Helen Keller that I could fix up and live in all by myself.

I'm not going to the Fall Festival next weekend, either.

—F.

To: Robert Wallop <wallop@dman.com>
From: Ayanna Bayo <ratlady@wz.org>
Received: Thursday, Oct. 23, 4:23 P.M.
Subject: Re: Stuff

Dear Frankie:

I don't know much about the Fall Festival, but your father made it sound like a big deal. Are you sure you want to miss it? Tell me what it's like.
    —A.

To: Ayanna Bayo <ratlady@wz.org>
From: Robert Wallop <wallop@dman.com>
Sent: Thursday, Oct. 23, 4:25 P.M.
Subject: Re: Stuff

Dear A.:

I don't *want* to miss the Fall Festival. It's sort of like the town's reason for being alive. The whole town comes together (along with some tourists) for a whole day full of traditions that we have to do exactly the same way every year because that's the way it is.

Before the sun rises, about one hundred people from Pepper Blossom meet in Maple County State Park at the top of Chestnut Hill for what's called the Sunrise Hum. My grandma Jenny always drives down from Michigan.

We all stand facing east in a huge huddle because it's always cold before the sun rises. All the trees around us are dark and sleepy. Then a sliver of gold begins to glow on the horizon, and that's when somebody starts the Hum. It's sort of a low "um" sound. Dad says it's like what the monks in Tibet do. Pretty soon everybody joins in, and the Hum gets louder and louder and higher and higher as more of the sun peeks out. And when the whole sun is visible in the sky, the Hum turns into what is called the Humdinger, which is like a big cheer. After that, we huddle around the grills and make pancakes and hot chocolate.

Then we have a parade and all sorts of contests and music in the town square for the rest of the day. At sunset we all go back to the state park and do the Sunset Hum, which is like the Sunrise Hum, only backward. Usually it's my favorite day of the year. Even better than Christmas.

There's no way I can go this year. Everybody will be teasing me about Johnny.

—F.

To: **Robert Wallop <wallop@dman.com>**
From: **Ayanna Bayo <ratlady@wz.org>**
Received: **Thursday, Oct. 23, 4:30 P.M.**
Subject: **Re: Stuff**

Dear Frankie:

I think you should go to the Fall Festival and try to have fun. If anybody teases you, don't pay attention. Remember an old African proverb: Ashes fly back in the face of those who throw them.

Yours,

Ayanna

To: Ayanna Bayo <ratlady@wz.org>
From: Robert Wallop <wallop@dman.com>
Sent: Thursday, Oct. 23, 4:31 P.M.
Subject: Re: Stuff

Dear Ayanna:
    You remind me of my favorite teacher, Ms.
Young. She always says wise things.
    —F.

To: Robert Wallop <wallop@dman.com>
From: Ayanna Bayo <ratlady@wz.org>
Received: Thursday, Oct. 23, 4:32 P.M.
Subject: Re: Stuff

Dear Frankie:
    I'll take that as a compliment.

To: **Ayanna Bayo <ratlady@wz.org>**
From: **Robert Wallop <wallop@dman.com>**
Sent: **Thursday, Oct. 23, 4:35 P.M.**
Subject: **Re: Stuff**

Dear Ayanna:

No offense, but I still think that naked mole-rats sound horrible. How the heck did you get interested in them in the first place? Why didn't you pick something cute, like koalas?

Curiously yours,
Frankie

To: **Robert Wallop <wallop@dman.com>**
From: **Ayanna Bayo <ratlady@wz.org>**
Received: **Thursday, Oct. 23, 4:40 P.M.**
Subject: **Re: Stuff**

Dear Frankie:

My father kept a vegetable plot behind our house in Kenya. When I was about Nutter's age, I noticed a small hill of dirt forming near the vegetables one early morning after a rain. I crept over and saw a spray of dirt being kicked up by some kind of little animal from below. I couldn't see the creature's face. In fact, all I could see was a scrawny, little, ugly, white butt.

I ran for my father. He explained how there are little creatures that live underground and eat crops from below. He ran to get a shovel. He, of course, wanted to open their tunnels and get them to leave his garden. I remember standing there in my little cotton dress, staring at the empty hole (our noise had scared the mole-rats deep into their tunnel), being both afraid and curious. Was there really a secret world of creatures digging under my feet? Part of me wanted to run away and the other part wished that I could become small enough to dive into the hole and see their underground home for myself.

After that, I read every book I could find about burrowing animals and insects. Often when I walked to school or to the village, I would try to imagine what the world under my feet must look like, all busy with unseen activity. I still do it when I'm walking in Rock Creek Park. Sometimes I even do it when I'm standing on the sidewalk in front of my apartment. Underneath all the concrete, if you dig deep enough, you find life! Somehow that makes me appreciate all life even more.

Deeply yours,

Ayanna

To: **Ayanna Bayo <ratlady@wz.org>**
From: **Robert Wallop <wallop@dman.com>**
Sent: **Thursday, Oct. 23, 4:42 P.M.**
Subject: **Re: Stuff**

Dear Ayanna:

What you wrote reminds me of Nutter. He has a thing for worms. He is abscessed with worms. He has to pick up every rock in order to see if there are worms squirming around in the mud underneath it.

I guess you figured out that Nutter and Skip don't have debilitating diseases. They are still annoying.

I've never thought about what is happening underground. But sometimes I stand still and imagine what it would be like to be deaf or blind. If I could *see* the creek splashing over the rocks and not hear it, would the creek look different? Would I see more colors in the water? If I could *hear* the treetops rustling in the wind and not see them, would the sound become visible inside my mind?

Thinking about what it would be like to be blind or deaf makes me appreciate what I see and hear even more.

Thoughtfully yours,
Frankie

To: **Robert Wallop <wallop@dman.com>**
From: **Ayanna Bayo <ratlady@wz.org>**
Received: **Thursday, Oct. 23, 4:45 P.M.**
Subject: **Re: Stuff**

Dear Frankie:

I can certainly relate to Nutter's obsession with worms.

What you wrote about trying to imagine being deaf or blind was so interesting. I'm going to be obsessed with thinking about it all day.

—A.

To: **Ayanna Bayo <ratlady@wz.org>**
From: **Robert Wallop <wallop@dman.com>**
Sent: **Thursday, Oct. 23, 4:51 P.M.**
Subject: **Re: Stuff**

Dear Ayanna:

Xnm,xnejheruopffam8794

Sorry. That was Nutter. He tried to pull me away from the computer. He keeps bugging me to help him with his koala costume, but I have no idea how to make a koala costume, and I have work to do. I absolutely must finish my science report right now. It's due tomorrow.

—F.

To: **Robert Wallop <wallop@dman.com>**
From: **Ayanna Bayo <ratlady@wz.org>**
Received: **Thursday, Oct. 23, 4:58 P.M.**
Subject: **Re: Stuff**

Dear Frankie:

You definitely should log off and do your homework. When you're finished with your report, here's an idea for Nutter's costume. Does he have a brown sweater? How about a white scarf tucked around his neck to look like the white fur around a koala's neck? I bet it wouldn't take much to make him *feel* like a koala—and that's all you need to do. Do you still have that stage paint kit? I'm sure he'd love to have his face painted. Try a mixture of brown and gray with a little black nose.

Hopefully helpfully yours,
Ayanna

To: **Ayanna Bayo <ratlady@wz.org>**
From: **Robert Wallop <wallop@dman.com>**
Sent: **Thursday, Oct. 23, 6:02 P.M.**
Subject: **Nutter**

Ayanna . . . are you on-line? The most horrible thing is happening. Nutter is missing, and it's my fault.

I don't know what to do.

—F.

Still Thursday, 6:10 P.M.

Dear Diary:

Nutter is missing. Dad and Skip went to look for him. I'm here going crazy.

I'll explain what happened.

After school I e-mailed Ayanna. Nutter kept bugging me about his costume, but I ignored him. Then I logged off, re-read Johnny's letter twenty times, and forced myself to start on my science report.

Dad came home from work early, and I thought he'd be happy to see me working so hard. But he was upset. He said that he got calls from the librarian, the nurse, Ms. Trolly, and Beth's mom.

"The librarian said you still haven't paid for the book," he said. "The nurse said you're missing classes. Ms. Trolly said that Johnny Nye wrote you an inappropriate note, and—"

"He did not write me an inappropriate note!" I yelled. "Jerry Parks forged that note."

"Frankie, don't raise your voice. We're going to talk about this calmly. Mrs. Jamison said that Beth came home from school very

195

upset today. She is worried about you. According to her you ditched school last Friday—"

"What a rat!"

"Ditched school, Frankie. That's serious."

"Everybody ditches."

"That's not true. Did you go to Johnny's trailer after school yesterday instead of coming home?"

"I hate Beth."

"Don't be mad at Beth, Frankie. She went to her mom for help. She talked to her about you because she thinks you're getting into trouble."

I pictured Beth pouring her heart out to her mom, and it made me feel even sicker.

"I want you to start at the beginning, Frankie, and tell me exactly what is going on."

Before I could figure out what to say, Skip ran in wanting to use the computer.

"Frankie and I are having a serious conversation," Dad said. "You and Nutter can watch TV until I call you."

"Where's Nutter?" Skip asked.

I was sort of happy to have a little distraction; but as soon as Skip asked about Nutter, I got the feeling something was wrong. The house was perfectly quiet. Uneasiness, black and inky, began to drip down the walls of my stomach.

Dad called upstairs. "Nutter?"

"I don't think he's inside," Skip said. He looked at me like he was feeling uneasy, too.

After we checked the basement, the attic, and the front and back yards, Skip finally said: "Maybe he went fishing."

"Fishing?" Dad's voice rose. "Why on Earth would he go fishing?"

Skip looked at me. He knew something, and he wouldn't say it.

Dad grabbed him by the shoulders. "What is it, Skip?"

"If I tell, I'm afraid that Frankie will take revenge on me."

"What?"

Skip broke down. "Frankie said she'd tell everybody that I wet my bed if I ever spied on her again."

I glared at Skip. He might as well have gotten a big old box of nails and hammered my coffin shut.

Dad exploded. "Out with it, Skip! Why did you say Nutter might be fishing?"

"Nutter kept bugging Frankie about making him a koala costume. She told him the only way to get a costume was to catch a magic fish that grants wishes."

Dad looked at me like I was insane.

Maybe I am insane. I don't know why I told that to Nutter. He was obsessing, and I wanted to get rid of him. That story popped into my mind because it's one of Nutter's favorite fairy tales. I remembered how our conversation ended:

"Frankie, take me fishing, please? Pretty please with Nutter Butter on top?"

"Go jump in a lake, Nutter. Can't you see I'm busy?"

"Frankie." Dad's voice was trying to be calm. "Did you tell Nutter to go fishing?"

"It was just something to say. I didn't think he'd take me seriously."

"So you just let him walk out the door?"

"It's not like I *let* him walk out the door. I didn't do anything."

"That's just it, Frankie. You didn't do anything. You were supposed to be baby-sitting." He turned to Skip. "Did you see him leave?"

"I saw him get mad at Frankie, but then I got busy."

"Probably busy spying on Mrs. Holmes," I yelled.

"That's enough, Frankie." He grabbed Skip. "Come on, we'll go to Pike's Pond. Frankie, you stay here in case he comes home."

The door slammed, and the house filled up with all the quiet of a graveyard.

Now I'm by myself, going absolutely crazy with worry. My mind is wandering between three dark scenes: The first is a picture of Nutter drowned in Pike's Pond; the second is a picture of Dad handing me over to the police with a look of disgust on his face; and the third is a picture of me pushing Skip off a cliff. Am I a horrible person because I'm feeling sorry for myself and hating Skip at a time like this? Shouldn't I be worrying only about

Nutter's safety? I think there's something really wrong with me. I know Dad wouldn't be thinking about himself at a time like this. Neither would Beth. Or Mrs. Holmes. Or even The Troll.

9:48 P.M.

It's all over. I don't think Dad will ever forgive me. I don't feel like writing; but I want to tell my side of the story, and nobody else wants to hear it.

After I wrote my last diary entry, I cried a whole bunch. Then I decided to stop feeling sorry for myself and do something positive. I imagined Dad coming home with Nutter. They'd be really hungry, so I decided to cook dinner. I'd have it all ready so that when they walked in the door, they'd smell something delicious. I put a frozen pizza in the oven and cleaned the living room and set the table. The kitchen timer buzzed. I was just about to take the pizza out when I heard a car and ran to the porch. Dad's friend Ozzie pulled up in his pickup truck.

"Did your dad find Nutter yet?" Ozzie asked. "I heard he's looking."

I shook my head.

"I'll keep my eye out," he said. "You know nothing bad could happen to Nutter in Pepper Blossom. Everybody's on the lookout." He waved and drove off.

What he said was supposed to make me feel better, but it made me feel worse. If Nutter had been hanging out on the banks of Pike's Pond, Dad would have found him already, and the call to look for Nutter wouldn't have gone out on the peppervine.

I pictured Nutter throwing his fishing line into the water, hoping for a magic fish, and it reminded me of the bridge over Dead Man's Creek. He wasn't at Pike's Pond. He was at Dead Man's Creek!

I almost ran out the door, and then I realized that Dad would be mad if he came home and found me missing. I wrote a very responsible note.

It was about 7:30. I had forgotten a jacket, but the night was warm. I passed a few people and asked them to keep an eye out for Nutter. I ran down the path that leads to the woods; the only sound was my feet pounding on the gravel and my voice whispering inside my head: *Please let Nutter be sitting on that bridge. Please let Nutter be sitting on that bridge.*

When I got to the woods, I had to stop and catch my breath. It was darker and cooler under the canopy of trees. The creek, which was high from all last week's rain, was rushing like it had someplace exciting to go and was in a hurry to get there.

I reached the bend and saw something on the bridge. I ran and stopped. Nutter's koala backpack.

"Nutter?" I called. The woods were quiet. The air had a deep green and gold smell. Above me I could sense the reds of the maples and the yellows of the oaks, even though the leaves were too dark to see. Below me the creek was tumbling over itself, glistening even in the dimness. If Nutter were hurt or dead, these woods and this creek wouldn't care.

They'd go on being beautiful. Nature is beautiful, but it doesn't care, does it? That's why people need each other. I thought about what Ayanna said about how lucky I am to have my family. She's right. I wouldn't want to be alone.

"Nutter?" I called again.

A sad little voice came from upstream. "That you, Frankie?"

He was crouching on the bank ahead, his feet and arms tucked in like a little turtle, his fishing pole next to him on the ground.

I rushed toward him. "Are you okay, Nutter?"

He kept looking at the ground, sniffling.

"Are you crying?"

He looked up at me, tears in his eyes. "I'm waiting for him to get better. And he's not."

A dead baby bird lay at his feet.

I crouched down. "You shouldn't have left the house, Nutter. We've been worried about you."

"I didn't catch a fish. But I did find rocks, and then I found this. . . ."

"It's really late, Nutter. We need to get home."

"I can hear him breathing," Nutter said.

I looked at the motionless bird. "I'm sorry, Nutter. The bird isn't breathing." I picked up a stick and very gently pushed on the bird's back. It was stiff.

Nutter took the stick and did what I did. "He *is* dead," he said sadly. "He's as dead as a rock, isn't he, Frankie?"

I stood and picked up his fishing pole. "Come on."

He stayed with the bird. "I bet I know why he died. I bet he was hungry because he didn't have a mom, and he came down and tried to lift up this rock to find some worms. But the rock was too heavy, and he died."

The little guy had a whole story figured out.

"We have to bury him," he insisted.

"Nutter, Dad's going to kill me. We have to get home."

He started digging a hole with the stick.

I sighed and put the fishing pole down. We dug a hole, gently pushed the bird in, and covered it up.

"Okay, Nutter. Now let's go home."

He didn't move. "We have to say a prayer."

I thought he wanted me to say a prayer, so I was rattling my brain trying to remember something appropriate; but then his clear, small voice streamed out, "O Bird, please be an angel and fly free. Over me. Amen." He smiled, happy that he had thought up just the right thing to say.

I picked up his fishing pole and took his hand.

"I didn't catch a fish, Frankie."

"I know."

"Will you help me make a koala costume anyway?"

I squeezed his hand. "As soon as we get home." I told him about the costume ideas that Ayanna had e-mailed, and he got excited.

All the way home, I kept thinking how happy Dad was going to be when he saw us. We finally got there and ran up the porch steps, and I opened the front door.

It took a few seconds for me to realize what was happening. Smoke billowed out.

"What's wrong?" Nutter yelled.

I pulled Nutter down the porch steps, and Mrs. Holmes came out of her house at the same time.

"Glory be!" she yelled. "There's smoke coming out your kitchen window."

She told us to stay outside and ran for the phone.

We stood in the front yard, our feet in the soft grass. I don't know what Nutter was thinking about. My mind was inside the house, imagining that the flames were eating up everything that I loved: photographs, dulcimers, this diary.

The fire truck came, and all the neighbors poured out to see if they could help. Ozzie's truck pulled up. Dad and Skip hopped out.

Dad's face was twisted like he couldn't figure out what was going on. He saw the smoke first and stumbled toward it. Then Nutter called out to him, and he turned and saw us. Before I could say anything, he ran over and picked Nutter up.

"You're okay," he said, and hugged Nutter close. Tears were streaming down his face. "You're okay, too, Frankie? Thank God!" He reached out and pulled me to him. And I started to cry because I knew that the only reason he cared about me was because he didn't yet know that the fire was my fault.

Chief Daniels stepped out onto the porch. "Not as bad as it looks, Robert," he boomed. "Just a kitchen fire. There's damage to a wall and those cabinets you've got over the oven—nothing you can't fix or paint. Didn't have time to spread beyond that. Soon as we get the smoke out, ya'll can go back in."

"We'll help," Ozzie said.

Dad was struggling to comprehend it.

"Started in the oven," the chief said. "You forget you were cooking something?"

Time went into slow motion. Dad set Nutter down and looked at me. "What happened, Frankie?"

Not a single lie came to my mind.

"I—I was making a pizza."

He shook his head slowly as if he couldn't believe what he was hearing. "You were making a pizza?"

The way he said it made it sound as if I was polishing my toenails.

I wanted to say that I was sorry and explain how thoughtful I was to make dinner for them, and how responsible I was to leave a note, and how smart I was to find Nutter. But I couldn't talk. Everybody was staring at me. My throat burned and my eyes were stinging. The air was growing cold.

"Frankie, what were you thinking?" he yelled. "First you lose Nutter, and then you almost burn down the house! You complain when I ask Mrs. Whitehead to look after you, and then you do something like this."

A car pulled up, and The Troll got out with a foil-covered pan.

"Doris Trolly!" Mrs. Holmes clapped her hands. "You came just in time. And with a little something, I see." She peered under the foil. "Lasagna for the Wallops. What a sweetheart you are!"

Something inside me snapped. "Would you mind your own business?" I yelled.

Everybody shut up. Mrs. Holmes looked at me as if I had slapped her across the face. The Troll looked at me as if she wanted to push me off the nearest bridge. Then the chief stepped out on the porch. "Robert, it's your phone. Somebody named Ayanna . . ."

Everybody looked at us, wondering what the heck that was about. I swear it was like a soap opera, except it wasn't at all funny.

Dad took the cordless phone. He said that he was busy and that he'd have to call back. She must have asked if everything was okay, because he sighed and said, "Yes, I just have a mess I have to clean up."

I'm the mess.

Chief Daniels let us back in after they blew out the smoke with some big fans. Behind and around and above the stove, everything was black: the ceiling, the cabinets, the light fixture. A whole wall full of Mom's postcards was burned. I knew them by heart. I knew which ones were now charred beyond recognition. Mount Everest at sunset. A Greek temple. The wild ponies at Chincoteague. A castle in Ireland. All gone. Nutter's favorite of a little Indian boy riding a baby elephant . . . gone.

I ran to my room.

I thought Dad would follow and yell. But he's too busy. A couple of people from church came over, and they're scrubbing down the kitchen.

Maybe I should go down and offer to help. My legs won't move.

I don't know how I'm going to sleep. I know I screwed up. I feel like crawling into a cave.

The house smells like a giant piece of burned toast.

11:06 P.M.

The phone rang at 10:30 P.M. Everybody was gone. Dad picked up in the kitchen.

I sat for a while in my bed, telling myself that it was wrong to listen in, but then I couldn't stand it. I crept out to the phone in the hallway and picked up the receiver. I think I have a sickness. A spy sickness. Maybe it's genetic. Maybe both Skip and I have it.

"What do you mean it's partly your fault?" Dad was asking.

"We were sending e-mail messages to each other after school." It was Ayanna. "Frankie should have been doing her homework and looking after Nutter instead of chatting with me on-line."

"E-mail messages about what?"

Ayanna was silent for a moment. "Various things. We've developed a sort of relationship."

"What do you mean?"

"I promised I wouldn't tell, Robert."

"What is this, some kind of secret?"

"No, not really. She e-mailed me. I e-mailed back. Now, she's opening up to me, writing more personal things."

"Personal things like what?"

"Today I think she needed some advice about, well, a boy."

"Johnny Nye?"

"Yes, I think so."

"And what advice did you give her?"

I didn't like the tone of his voice. I don't think Ayanna did, either.

"I think you should talk with Frankie about this, Robert, because—"

"Well, I think I have the right to know what you've been talking with Frankie about."

"We talked about how cruel kids can be sometimes and how sometimes you have to stand up for what's right."

"So you encouraged her to . . . ?"

"I encouraged her to be true to her heart."

Dad was silent. "Ayanna, I'm sure you meant well. But you don't know Frankie. And you don't know Johnny Nye. You don't know what's going on here. I don't think you should be interfering and trying to give advice long distance."

"I'm sorry, Robert. I didn't mean to interfere. It seemed like she was reaching out to me—"

"She shouldn't be reaching out to a stranger who lives six hundred miles away. She should be reaching out to me. Or to her guidance counselor. Someone who's here. She's been getting into trouble. Did you know? Serious trouble. She ditched school. Forged a note. Rumors are flying about her and this boy. I thought he was basically a good kid, but now I'm not sure. She's lying and cheating. She never used to do this."

"I don't think it's because of the boy—"

"How do you know?" he snapped, and then his voice grew soft. "I'm sorry, Ayanna. I don't want to be angry with you. It's just that I'm very frustrated right now. I think I got so caught up with what was happening with you that I forgot to pay attention to what was happening here at home. I let things get out of control."

There was a long silence. I held my breath, afraid that they would hear me.

"Perhaps we should step back," Dad finally said.

"It's always wise to be cautious," Ayanna agreed.

"Maybe it was a crazy idea—you and me," Dad said. "We're worlds apart."

She didn't say anything.

Dad took a deep breath. "I'll call you once things get straightened out around here."

"Okay," she said.

It didn't sound like either of them believed it.

Midnight

I want to e-mail Ayanna. I want to tell her that none of this is her fault. But I'm too nervous. If Dad catches me on-line, he'll have a nervous breakdown for real.

Friday, October 24, 11:00 A.M.

Dear Diary:

I can't get out of bed. The whole house still stinks like a bad report card with my name on it.

Dad came in at 7:30, and I rolled over to face the wall.

"Frankie, at some point we'll need to talk about what happened last night. For now you should know that I'm grounding you for a week. No friends. No phone calls."

No problem, I thought. No friends anyway.

"No e-mailing either," he said. "Now get moving or you'll be late."

"I'm not going." I pulled the covers over my head.

He yanked them off. "You're not going to miss another day of school."

"I'm sick."

"Stop lying, Frankie!"

"I can't go to school."

"You can, and you will."

I pulled the covers back on. "You can't make me, Dad. I really am sick to my stomach."

"Fine!" he shouted. "But if you stay home from school today, then I'm calling Ms. Trolly, and I'm telling her that I give up. She can come after school every day next week and give you the benefit of her guidance. I actually think it would be very good for you. And me."

"I don't care. Just don't make me go to school today."

He left in a huff.

I'm never getting out of bed again. I'm starved, but I can't face the kitchen.

10:00 P.M.

Dad didn't even try talking. He hates me. Everybody probably hates me.

Ayanna probably hates me for getting her into trouble. Johnny probably hates me because he thinks I hate him. Even Nutter probably hates me for burning up his favorite postcard.

Saturday, October 25, 9:16 P.M.

I woke up to the smell of paint and the sound of a vacuum. I pulled the covers over my head, intending to stay here all day, when Nutter came in.

"She's here," he whispered. "Dad's gone, and she's here."

Right away I knew something was wrong. He pulled me out of bed and over to the staircase. He pointed down.

Pushing the vacuum over our living room carpet was none other than The Troll.

Nutter pulled me back into my room. "Dad had to go to the shop, and she's going to be here all day," he explained. "We have to clean the whole house, and we can't play until it's done. She sent me to wake you up. She said it's 'high' time. What's 'high' time?"

"Forget it, Nutter," I said.

I walked down to get some breakfast, and she waved at me as if she's always at our house on Saturday mornings, vacuuming.

"Good morning, Francine," she chirped. "I'm saving the hallway rugs for you."

I felt like saying it was high time for her to leave.

In the kitchen, the stove was disconnected. Ozzie was scraping the remains of the postcards off the wall behind it. Bits and pieces of blackened paper and ash fluttered to the floor with each scrape. The sound went straight to my heart like a knife. It was like having an operation without being put to sleep first.

The Troll had Skip scrubbing the kitchen floor. If I didn't hate him, I would have felt sorry for him.

"Hey, Frankie," Ozzie said when he noticed me. "The kitchen is out of order. But there's coffee cake from Mrs. Holmes in the dining room."

We cleaned all morning. The Troll was in heaven. She loves to clean. When we were done, she even vacuumed the vacuum.

At lunch, she made us all sit down and talk about how we could better communicate as a family. Then she told Nutter and Skip to "play a cooperative game together." She told me I had to finish my report and that she would help me, if I needed it.

"What is the topic?" she asked.

"Naked mole-rats," I said.

Her face screwed itself into a question mark. Clearly she had never heard of naked mole-rats.

When I finished the report, she said she would read it "for errors." She didn't find any. She wouldn't know one if it bit her in the face.

"I know an expert on naked mole-rats," I said. "I'll e-mail it to her to check."

She shook her head like The Troll that she is and said: "Your father said no e-mailing."

I was appalled. I wanted to snort and stamp my feet and butt her out of the house with my head. I locked myself in my room and re-read Johnny's letter twenty more times, and that just made me feel worse.

At dinner she pulled out this gigantic beef casserole that she had brought to "pop" into the microwave. I told her that we're all vegetarians, and you should have seen her face fall down. I knew I'd get into trouble for it later, but it was worth it.

Dad came home from work and went crazy about how great the house looked. He thanked The Troll twelve million times, and then he invited her to stay for dinner. She apologized about making beef and said that if she'd have known, she would have made a vegetable casserole.

He told her that he and Skip and Nutter loved beef, and then he glared at me.

Beth didn't call today. She always calls on Saturdays. I guess that's the end of our friendship. Since she ratted on me, I should be happy that it's the end.

I'm so depressed, I could drop dead.

I wonder what Johnny did all day.

The Red Beet Ramblers are playing in the living room right now, and I am locked in my room wishing that I had earplugs.

I've been here practically all day. I stayed in bed this morning and refused to go to church. Dad said he didn't have the strength to argue.

While he and Skip and Nutter were at church, I went down to the basement and looked at the dulcimer. He hadn't touched it. I put the silver tuning pegs back where I'd found them.

After church Dad went to Heartstrings, and—surprise—Grandma Jenny came.

"I'm staying the whole week!" she said.

Dad didn't say so, but he must have asked her to come so that he could avoid me. We wouldn't fight in front of her. We never do. She's not the kind of grandma you can fight in front of. We wouldn't get into any deep conversations, either. She's not the kind of grandma who wants to know how you're feeling. She's a chocolate-chip cookie kind of grandma. A card-playing kind of grandma. A "say cheese" kind of grandma.

She made cookies and played games with Nutter and Skip all afternoon. I am still too angry at Skip to be in the same room as him. She asked me to join, but she didn't make a big deal when I said that I had too much homework (which was a lie).

After dinner the Red Beet Ramblers squashed into the living room, and I locked myself back in my room because I couldn't face them.

Dad knocked on my door. "Time for rehearsal, Frankie."

"I'm not coming."

"If you want to lock yourself in here, that's fine," he said. "But if you don't rehearse, then you can't play with us at the festival."

"Fine," I said.

Now they're playing "Give Me Your Hand," and it's killing me.

Grandma just came up to say good night.

"You know that you have to go to school tomorrow, Frankie," she said, matter of fact. "Grin and bear it. You can't hide in your room for the rest of your life."

I don't know why not.

To: **Ayanna Bayo <ratlady@wz.org>**
From: **Robert Wallop <wallop@dman.com>**
Sent: **Monday, Oct. 27, 3:46 P.M.**
Subject: **Sorry**

Dear Ayanna:

I'm not supposed to be e-mailing, but I can't help it. I think I got you into trouble with my dad. I'm sorry. Nothing was your fault. He shouldn't hold anything against you.

I got through school by imagining that if I took my eyes off my teachers, or stopped listening to them for a single second, the entire world would blow up.

During passing periods, I avoided everybody, and everybody avoided me. At lunch, Beth sat with the other seventh-graders who are on stage crew. I sat by myself on one side of the cafeteria. Out of the corner of my eye, I could see Johnny sitting by himself. He looked as miserable as I felt.

I keep thinking about what you said about being true to your heart. I wanted to walk over and sit with him, but I didn't. I'm a coward.

At least nobody teased us. It was like somebody had told everybody that they'd get into trouble if they teased me or Johnny. Maybe it was The Troll.

Turned in my report on naked mole-rats.

Yours truly,

Frankie

To: **Robert Wallop <wallop@dman.com>**
From: **Ayanna Bayo <ratlady@wz.org>**
CC: **Robert Wallop <dulcimerman@ dman.com>**
Received: **Monday, Oct. 27, 4:00 P.M.**
Subject: **Re: Sorry**

Dear Frankie:

Thank you for your e-mail. But I have to tell you that I can't continue our correspondence. Your dad and I talked on the phone about the situation. I don't want to interfere any more than I already have.

I'm sending a copy of this to your dad's business e-mail address so that there are no secrets between us.

I hope you know how much I have enjoyed getting to know you. I know that you are going to figure out what you need to do to get through these difficult times. I think you're an extraordinary girl, Frankie Wallop.

Best wishes,
Ayanna

Monday, Oct. 27, 4:10 P.M.

Dear Diary:
I hate Dad.

Tuesday, October 28, 7:04 P.M.

Dear Diary:
I finally gave the librarian the money for *The Miracle Worker.* She must have assumed

that I lost the book because she said, "Well, if it turns up, bring it in, honey."

Right.

Got a B on my report. Would have gotten an A, but Mrs. Keating deducted points for being late. She liked it so much she made me read it out loud. Jerry Parks laughed every time I said the word *naked*. Some people are so immature.

All day Johnny looked like a squashed tomato. He's waiting for me to write back to tell him that I don't hate him. I wrote him a letter, but then I threw it away.

After school The Troll called to check up on me. "I know you're going through a difficult time right now, Francine. Your father and I talked about the possibility of after-school counseling sessions—"

I stopped her flat. "My grandmother is here for a while, so we don't need anything."

She paused, clearly disappointed. Then she said, "That's so nice. I'd like to introduce myself to her. Could you put her on please, Frankie?"

I handed the phone over.

"That woman could talk your ear off," Grandma Jenny said when she finally hung up.

Wednesday, October 29, 4:30 P.M.

Dear Diary:
Johnny wasn't in school today.
Too depressed to write.

8:15 P.M.

Nutter just came into my room. "Grandma's having coffee at Mrs. Holmes's house. Will you read me a book?"

"I don't feel like it, Nutter. I'm busy." I was sitting in my beanbag chair, staring at the lines on my left palm.

He huffed. "This is a zombie house."

I glanced up. He had his hands on his hips and a disgusted look on his face. "What do you mean?" I asked.

"Everybody just walks around. Nobody talks to each other. It's worse than a zombie house. It's a dead zombie house." He stormed out.

Dear Diary:

This morning Mr. Peter asked me to take the attendance sheets to the office. On the way I ran into Johnny, who was coming in late. Nobody else was in the hallway.

He stopped when he saw me. He had no books. No backpack. He had on jeans that were ripped at both knees. His eyes were waiting.

My heart was thumping as loudly as Ozzie Filmore's boots do when he plays "Soldier's Joy" on the fiddle. *Say something. Say something. Say, Hello, Johnny.*

The door to Mrs. Bourne's room opened, and Denise walked out.

My feet took off toward the office. I don't know what Johnny did. I couldn't look back.

Went to the nurse's office. She wouldn't let me stay. "It's either back to class or in to talk to Ms. Trolly. Sorry. Your dad gave me orders."

I went back to class and imagined that I was deaf and blind.

I'm at lunch right now, and I'm still deaf and blind. I can't hear the clock ticking. I can't see everyone sitting with friends.

It is remarkable that I am able to write in this diary. For a blind person my handwriting is excellent. I am an extraordinary girl.

9:30 P.M.

I've been so wrapped up in my own worries, I forgot about Nutter.

After school the poor little guy was in tears when I picked him up.

"Lindsay's mom made her a whole elephant costume with a trunk. You still haven't helped me with my costume," he said. "Every day you say that you'll help me tomorrow. Tomorrow is Halloween, Frankie. Grandma says I should wear rags and be a bum. I don't want to be a bum, Frankie."

I took his hand.

As soon as we arrived home, I went to work. I found a white handkerchief and an old winter coat of mine (furry and brown!). I tied the handkerchief around his neck and put the coat on him. Already he looked like a little teddy bear. Then I pulled out the stage paint kit and I painted his face. When he looked in the mirror, he squealed. Ayanna was right. It didn't take much to make him *feel* like a koala. He put on his koala backpack and danced around and around the house.

I wish I were five years old again. I wish that putting on a costume and dancing around the room could make everything all right.

Took a picture of him with Dad's electronic camera. Want to send it to Ayanna but am afraid it would get her into trouble.

Friday, October 31, 5:10 P.M.

Dear Diary:

At lunch Beth plopped her bag on the table and sat next to me.

"Johnny told Jerry Parks that he hates you and that you hate him and that the reason you came over last week was for business," she began. "He said that you paid him to teach you how to find some music that your dad needed on the Internet."

I stared at my half-peeled orange. Johnny was lying for me. Johnny had given up.

Beth scooted her chair in. "I think you tried to tell me all that last week, and I didn't believe you."

I didn't say anything.

She kept going. "I didn't know what to believe because you lied to me. You haven't ever lied to me before. I know you're really mad at me for telling my mom everything, but I didn't know what else to do. I thought you were in trouble. Please talk to me, Frankie. Tell me what you're thinking."

Here's what I was thinking: I know Beth inside and out. I know every freckle on her face. I know that one eye is rounder than the other. I know how loud she screamed when she got her ears pierced at the mall in Bloomington. I know what she wishes she had been named. I know that she has a white scar on her left knee and that she got it ice-skating. I was there. I tied my scarf around her knee to stop the bleeding.

I was thinking that all I had to do to make things right with Beth was say, Everything is okay. All I needed to do was say, I forgive you for telling your mom and I'm sorry for lying and, yes, I hate Johnny and he hates me.

Out of the corner of my eye, I could see Johnny, sitting alone near the garbage cans. He was working on something in his notebook, but he kept glancing over. He was waiting to see if Beth and I were going to make up.

I should tell Beth the truth, I thought. I should tell her what Johnny's really like. I should tell her that I'm going to be his friend, whether she thinks it's okay or not. I could do it. All I had to do was get up and walk over to Johnny's table. *Hello, Johnny.* That was all I needed to say. It was the right thing to do. Pretending to hate Johnny would be a lie.

The pressure to tell the truth was hanging over my head like ten thousand pounds of tomatoes. But the pressure to lie was just as huge.

I didn't move.

"Earth to Frankie . . ." Beth was staring at me. "Did you hear me? I said: Do you think things can get back to normal?"

I nodded. "Sure, Beth."

The bell rang. I walked out with Beth and didn't look back. I mumbled and lied my way through an apology, and things sort of did get back to normal. Beth went with me to pick up Nutter after school and to see all the elementary kids dressed up in their costumes. We went back to my house and carved jack-o'-lanterns with Skip and Nutter and Grandma. Beth and I pretended that everything was fine between us, but there was an awkwardness that wasn't there before. She went home a few minutes ago.

I thought that writing this down would make me feel better. But it doesn't. I keep picturing Johnny alone in his trailer on Endangered Species Road, and it makes my stomach hurt.

10:38 P.M.

I did not imagine that Halloween night would end this way. How could I?

After Beth left, I fell into the darkest depression yet. First of all, I felt like a monster. How could I turn my back on Johnny? Secondly, I was a fake. How could I pretend that things were normal with Beth when I couldn't tell her what was really going on? Thirdly, I was still obsessing about what happened last week. How could I ever forgive myself for allowing Nutter to wander off, or for almost burning down the house (the kitchen still doesn't smell right), or for getting Ayanna into trouble?

On top of it all, there was the whole trick-or-treat thing. Beth wanted to go. I said no because I felt too old. This is true—I do feel too old, and that makes me sad—but it's not the whole truth. The whole truth is that I was too depressed to go, but I couldn't explain that. So for the first time in the history of my life, I spent the night watching TV in the family room while Dad took Nutter and Skip trick-or-treating. When they got home, Skip tried to make up with me by giving me some of his candy. Big sacrifice. He had a whole pillowcase full.

Later, while Grandma was putting Nutter and Skip to bed, Dad came in and asked me if I would mind turning off the TV so that we could "talk." He had this nice voice, but I could tell that he wasn't asking. Why do kids have to "talk" whenever grown-ups want? I hit the OFF button on the remote and promptly turned into a dead zombie.

"I spoke with Doris Trolly today," he said brightly. "She said that you've had an excellent week at school. You paid for the library book. You did all your work and stayed focused."

That's what a dead zombie does best, I thought.

He pulled over a chair and sat down. "And I was glad to hear that Beth came over today. I think that's a step in the right direction."

Goody-goody. The dead zombie is stepping in the right direction.

"Look," he said. "Tomorrow is the Fall Festival. I know what I said last Sunday about your not playing. But it only comes once a year, and it's such a special ritual, and I've been thinking—"

"I'm staying home tomorrow, Dad."

"Staying home?" He sighed. "Frankie, what's going on? Ms. Trolly said—"

"Ms. Trolly can jump off a bridge." I stood up.

"Sit back down, Frankie."

I started walking away.

"Do *not* lock yourself in your room, Frankie. I'm warning you. I've let this go on for too long. We are going to sit down and talk about this in a calm, rational . . ."

I left his sentence dangling in midair. I ran upstairs and slammed my bedroom door.

A few seconds later he pounded on my door. "Open up, Frankie!"

I heard Grandma Jenny's voice. "Robert, what in heaven's name?"

"I'm having it out with Frankie, Mom. Just stay out of it." He pounded again.

"I don't want to talk!" I shouted. "Leave me alone."

"Unlock this door right now or else—"

"Or else what?"

Silence. Then I heard him marching down the stairs.

I sat on my beanbag chair and pulled my pillow on top of me. I could feel the fringe of the pillowcase brushing against my arm.

A few minutes later he came back and started making noise. My first thought was that he was adding a lock on the outside so that I couldn't get out. But then the sound of his electric screwdriver jolted the air, and the door started to wiggle.

"What are you doing?" I yelled.

The door wiggled more; and then Dad was standing there, holding the door in his hands.

"You can't take my door off."

He set the door against the hallway wall. "I just did."

The doorway looked big and naked and stupid without its door. It made me feel big and naked and stupid. "Put it back!" I yelled. "I should be allowed some privacy."

"You can't lock yourself in this room and refuse to talk, Frankie. We are a family. We have to at least try to communicate."

I threw myself on my bed and pulled the pillow over my face.

He sat on my bed. "Ms. Trolly suggested that we each have a turn to say everything we want to say." He was out of breath. I guess ripping doors from their frames takes some effort. "When you're talking I promise to listen; and when I'm talking, you have to promise to listen. I think that sounds like a good idea. What do you think?"

"I think Ms. Trolly should win a goody-goody award for all her good ideas."

"Stop it, Frankie. You're being mean and sarcastic. I'm trying to help here. You need to meet me halfway. Take that pillow off your face and look at me."

I huffed and sat up.

"Thank you," he said. "Now, do you want to go first or should I?"

"You seem ready to go."

"All right." He scooted back on my bed and crossed his legs, Indian style. Beth always goes on and on about how handsome my dad is. She likes his beard. He doesn't look handsome to me. He just looks like a dad, a highly annoying dad.

"Okay," he said. "Here's what the last two weeks look like from my perspective."

This was going to be fun.

"I come home from my trip to D.C., and everything's fine. Then strange things start to happen. First, you tell Mrs. Holmes that it's your birthday. Then you tell me that Mrs. Holmes has Alzheimer's."

I forgot about that one.

"Then you refuse to be in the school play. Then you rip up a library book. Then you let Nutter eat half a cake. When I try to talk, you lock yourself in your room. When I threaten to hire a baby-sitter, you promise to watch Nutter more closely and pay for the book.

Meanwhile, everybody in Pepper Blossom is being extra nice to me because you told Mr. Haxer that I'm having a nervous breakdown."

I wonder how he found out about that one.

"Then I find out that you've been accused of cheating, that you didn't pay for the book, that you haven't been doing your homework, and that you've been hanging out with Johnny Nye. You insist that you didn't cheat, that you've been working on your report, and that you haven't been hanging out with Johnny; and then you promise to pay for the book. I think all is well. The very next day I get four phone calls at work. I hear that you're hiding in the nurse's office, that you went to Johnny Nye's trailer—"

"I told you—"

"It's my turn to talk, Frankie. When I'm done, then you can say whatever you want."

I bit my lip so hard it almost bled. It was horrible hearing a list of my sins. It was like each one was a dart, and I was the dartboard. Why was he just listing *my* sins? Why not his? Why not Nutter's? Why not Skip's?

"I also hear that you ditched school the week before," he continued. "But we never get to talk about these issues because Nutter runs away from home and you set the kitchen on fire."

"I didn't set—"

"Then you basically lock yourself in your room again. You won't talk. You won't look me in the eye. You glare at Skip. You ignore Nutter. And I hear that you won't even talk to your best friend." He sighed. "Now, like I said, I'm glad to see some improvement. You helped Nutter with his Halloween costume. That was very nice. And you seem to have patched things up with Beth. But I'm still very, very worried."

I was so angry I was shaking. "You don't understand."

"I know I don't!" he said. "I don't understand any of it. But I want to understand, so please explain it."

Everything that had happened, all the things he listed and more were exploding in my head like bombs. How could I explain? I pulled the pillow back on top of me.

"Come on, Frankie. Let it out."

I was afraid that if I started to talk, I'd cry.

"I want to hear whatever you want to say, Frankie. And I promise I'll listen."

The way he said it reminded me of The Troll. I smacked the pillow against the wall. "You don't want to know what I have to say. You don't care about me. You don't ever listen to me. You don't ever believe me."

"How can I believe you when you've been avoiding me and lying to me and keeping secrets?"

"You've been avoiding me, too. You've been lying and keeping secrets. You even ditched, didn't you? You ditched your meetings to be with Ayanna. Why haven't you said anything about her, Dad? When I asked you who the dulcimer is for, why did you say, 'Nobody special'? What were you planning to do, move us to Washington? Or let her move in here and change everything that Mom did? Did you ever think that I might not want to move or share my life with somebody I don't even know?"

My dad's face went as blank as a white

sheet. He leaned back against the wall and closed his eyes. Neither of us said anything for a minute. I was still shaking, not so much from anger anymore as from the shock of having said so much so fast. The air in the room felt different. It was as if I had blasted through a huge barrier that had been between us, only I couldn't tell if it was a good thing or a bad thing. I pulled the pillow into my lap so that there'd be something between us again.

"I don't know why I didn't tell you about Ayanna," he finally said. "It was all so new, and it was all happening so quickly. I didn't know what to say."

"So you didn't say anything?"

He opened his eyes and looked at me, really looked at me. "You're right, Frankie. I was avoiding you and keeping secrets. I should have talked to you about it. But I didn't know where it was going, and it felt awkward. How could I tell my daughter that I was falling in love?" His voice started to fall apart. His eyes filled with tears. "I never thought I'd have to. I never thought I'd lose your mom."

I couldn't look at him. I closed my eyes and pressed the pillow against my face and chest.

"Frankie, do you know how much I loved your mom? She was the wonder of the world. She could make me laugh so hard that my face hurt for weeks. I miss her every day. I'll never stop missing her." I could tell he was crying by the sound of his voice. "Don't you know that?"

I couldn't breathe, but it wasn't from the pillow. It was from the lump in my throat.

He reached over and gently pulled the pillow away. Tears were streaming down his face. "I would never ask someone to marry me before you had the chance to meet her, Frankie. I would never let anybody move in here and change everything that Mom did. I love you, Frankie. Do you believe me?"

I nodded.

He hugged me so tight that I could feel his heart beating, and he didn't let go. He smelled like a tree. His beard was wet against my ear.

I didn't breathe or move or blink. I held myself still because I was afraid that if I started to cry, I would never stop. Over his shoulder I saw the glow-in-the-dark stars dangling from the ceiling above my bed. They glistened and danced because I was seeing them through all the tears that I was busy trying to keep from pouring out of my eyes. In a rush I remembered all the nights that Mom and I would lie together and look up at those stars and talk. I remembered the way her laugh always sounded like wind blowing through curtains, and I couldn't hold it in anymore. I started to cry, and Dad held me tighter.

"I miss her so much," I cried.

"What do you miss most?"

"I miss the way you guys used to stand in my doorway every night and sing 'Twinkle, Twinkle' in harmony."

We cried for a while together. Then he asked me if I could breathe and I had to laugh.

We both sat back and wiped our faces. It crossed my mind that Grandma and Nutter and Skip probably heard everything. I didn't care.

It must have crossed Dad's mind, too, because he yelled out, "Mom, Skip, Nutter . . .

get in here right now. We have something to talk about."

Nutter and Skip appeared in the open doorway in their pajamas, looking like two lost sheep. Grandma Jenny's eyes were all teary, and she was blowing her nose.

"Come on in," Dad said. He opened his arms, and Nutter scampered onto his lap. Skip sat down right where he was, and Grandma perched on the bed.

"As you probably heard, Frankie and I were talking about how much we miss your mom," he said to Skip and Nutter.

"I miss her, too," Skip said.

He was sitting with his knees hugged to his chest, half in and half out of my room, looking very alone.

"What do you miss most, Skip?" Dad asked.

"I miss the way she'd always be waiting for me at the flagpole after school. I miss walking with her. She always told jokes."

I thought about how fast Skip always runs home now, how much in a hurry he always seems to be.

Dad reached over and pulled Skip in for a hug.

"I don't even know what to miss," Nutter wailed. "I don't have any rememories."

Grandma leaned forward. "I remember when you were born, Nutter. You got the hiccups right away, and they wouldn't stop. You were just this little round bundle with big brown eyes, going *hiccup, hiccup, hiccup.*"

Nutter grinned.

"And that's when your mother nicknamed you. What a little Nutter, she said. She loved you so much. She loved all of you so much."

Nutter jumped up and hugged her.

"Now, I want all of you to hear this so that there aren't any misunderstandings," Dad said. "I went on a few dates with a woman in Washington, D.C."

This was news to Grandma. Her eyebrows jumped way up.

"The naked mole-rat lady," Nutter explained.

Dad laughed. "Her name is Ayanna Bayo. She is the keeper of the naked mole-rats at the National Zoo. It was very nice. And who knows, someday I might go on another date with somebody else. But if I do, that doesn't mean I'm going to get married. I promise that from now on I'll let you guys know if I start to date anyone. And I want you to know that you can ask me anything, anytime."

"Are you going to marry The Troll?" Nutter asked.

Dad laughed. "No, I'm not going to marry Doris Trolly. Boy, you guys have wild imaginations."

"Well, she wants to marry you," Skip said.

"She does not," Dad scoffed.

"Oh, yes she does," Grandma said, and we all looked at her, surprised.

Dad turned red. I don't think I'd ever seen him blush.

Grandma smiled at me and said, "Men are always the last to know."

Dad stood up. "Well, now that we've got that all cleared up, I think it's time for you boys to get to bed. Remember, tomorrow's the festival, so we're getting up *before* dawn. Come on. Mom and Frankie, we're going to sing."

Skip and Nutter hopped into their beds. Grandma and Dad and I stood in their doorway and sang "Twinkle, Twinkle" in harmony, except that I had to stop singing halfway through because of the lump in my throat. I had this feeling that Mom was there, singing with us. And although I felt sad, I felt really happy, too.

"I've got a bedtime story to finish reading," Grandma told Dad. "So why don't you and Frankie go down and have dessert? I made pumpkin cupcakes."

"Give you a lift," Dad said, turning his back to me and crouching down.

"I'm too big." I laughed and hopped on his back.

He groaned and then galloped down the stairs.

We sat at the kitchen table and talked over cupcakes and milk. I started at the beginning. I told him how I'd found that first e-mail and how one lie led to another. I told him how much I hated Ratlady, and how I went to Johnny's trailer to learn how to hack into his business e-mail.

"You can't blame Johnny," I said. "He didn't do anything wrong. Don't listen to Doris Trolly, Dad. She really is a troll."

He laughed so hard he almost spit out his milk.

"Johnny didn't write me any nasty letter. He isn't a bad influence at all. He is really sweet and smart. Remember what you said, Dad, that he's got a lot more going for him than people in this town realize? That he could use a friend?"

He nodded. "I've always liked Johnny. But I got worried. When I heard that you were hanging around with him and getting into trouble, I thought maybe he was the cause of it."

"He wasn't. Promise you won't hold anything against him or worry about it anymore? He really admires you."

"I promise. I won't worry anymore." He smiled and shook his finger at me. "But if you start dating, you have to tell me. I don't want to hear it from Mrs. Holmes."

I laughed.

"And you don't have to worry about Ayanna, Frankie. I don't think that's going to work out." He wiped some crumbs off the table and took them to the sink. Behind him, the new white paint on the wall glistened blankly.

Ayanna.

After all these days it was strange to talk about her out loud. When did I stop calling her Ratlady? I thought about the letter that Dad had written, the one that he had asked me to mail, the one that I had ripped up in math class. *You're like the sun coming up in the morning, Ayanna. Everything about you shines with warmth and light. Even your e-mails.*

I wiped the crumbs off my side of the table. "It's not her fault, you know," I said. "She didn't do anything wrong."

He turned around and surrendered a sad smile. "Well, it doesn't matter. I don't think any of us are ready for any big changes."

I pictured us—Dad, Skip, Nutter, and me—scurrying around in our own little dark tunnel system. I pictured Ayanna, scurrying around in her own little dark tunnel system. I pictured all the miles and miles of hard, dark earth in between.

I got up and dumped my handful of crumbs into the sink. "You know what Ayanna says, Dad? She says that change can be good. Change can help you grow."

He smiled. "That sounds like Ayanna."

We didn't talk much longer. Dad ordered me to bed because he said there was no way I was going to miss the Fall Festival tomorrow. He walked me upstairs, and there was my bedroom door off its hinges in the hallway.

He gave me a funny smile. "I forgot about that." He whispered so he wouldn't wake up Nutter and Skip.

I walked into my room and noticed how different it felt without the door. So open.

"I'll put that back on tomorrow if you promise not to lock it again," he whispered.

"Okay," I said, and climbed into bed.

"What about pajamas?"

I shrugged. "We have to get up so early, I might as well sleep in my clothes."

He laughed and turned out the light. Then he came back over and pulled my blanket up to my chin like I was a kid again. "I'm tucking you in, little Frankie," he said, patting down my blanket. He sat on the side of my bed in the dark and sang "Twinkle, Twinkle." Then he kissed me good night and went downstairs.

It was goofy, but it felt good to be tucked in.

I should have gone to sleep, but I had to get up and write. I'm sitting at my desk by the window.

There are no clouds. The stars are bright.

To: **Ayanna Bayo <ratlady@wz.org>**
From: **Robert Wallop <wallop@dman.com>**
Sent: **Saturday, Nov. 1, 10:34 P.M.**
Subject: **Fall Festival**

Dear Ayanna:

My dad said that it's okay for me to write to you. I have to tell you what happened at the Fall Festival, which was today.

First my dad woke us up while it was still dark and piled us into the car: Nutter, Skip, Grandma Jenny, and me. It was too early to talk. We just sat and looked out the windows at the sleeping world.

At first I was excited to be going. But when we got to the top of Maple County State Park, where everybody was gathering, I felt nervous. All sorts of neighbors, teachers, and kids that I felt uncomfortable around were there: Beth, Mr. Haxer, Melinda Bixby, Mrs. Holmes, and that woman I told you about called The Troll, to name a few.

I sandwiched myself between my grandma Jenny and Nutter, and imagined that I was inside a balloon, watching everything happen.

The sky grew lighter and lighter, and then a sliver of pale yellow appeared on the horizon, and somebody started the Hum.

Everybody stood in a huddle, humming softly, watching the sliver grow into a ball of fire. It was probably beautiful, but I wasn't really paying attention. My dad was standing just a little in front of me. The light was hitting his face, making his beard look more reddish. Even though he was standing in a big huddle, surrounded by people, he looked alone. He was staring at the sun, and I know what he was thinking about. He was thinking about you, Ayanna.

I looked around and noticed all the people who weren't there. I know that probably sounds strange.

But I used to think that everybody came to the park to do the Hum, and I noticed for the first time that it's not true. The people who come to the Hum are the same people who run the town. It's the same people who sponsor the Christmas Tree Lighting, and organize the Fourth of July, and everything else. They're the people who have money—not a lot, nobody here's a millionaire—but enough.

Maybe there are different colonies in Pepper Blossom, just like there are with naked mole-rats. We're in one colony. The Hum Colony. And in another colony are people like Johnny and his grandma, people who live in trailers or in ramshackle houses with no washer and dryer. The colonies don't cross paths very often.

Does it have to be that way? Do Johnny and his grandma stay away from the Hum because they want to, or because they've never been invited? If they stay away because they haven't been invited, then why doesn't somebody just invite them? I think that in order for a tradition to be really beautiful, it should be something that everybody shares.

The Hum was getting louder and louder, turning into an "ah" sound. When the sun cleared the horizon and everybody cheered, mine came out more like a croak.

During breakfast Mrs. Jamison put me in charge of pouring hot chocolate, and it was nice to have something to do. The Troll planted herself next to my dad at one of the pancake grills and wouldn't budge. Dad looked highly uncomfortable.

"Should we rescue him?" I asked Grandma.

"He's got to learn these things himself," she said.

Nobody said anything to me about all the trouble I had gotten into, but Ozzie and Chief Daniels started teasing me about the fire. I was actually glad that they did because it made the whole thing seem less serious.

"I hear it started in the oven, Frankie," Ozzie said. "You're going to need some cooking lessons if you ever want to get married."

"Well, I don't know about that," Chief Daniels said. "She cooks as good as my Betsy."

Everybody laughed, and Betsy Daniels said, "Well, I think Frankie is going to marry a man who cooks for *her*." And all the women around cheered. I like Ozzie and the Daniels family. They seem happy all the time, so they must be doing something right.

"Speaking of marriage," Mr. Haxer said, "I have something I'd like to announce." He stood on a bench and addressed the whole crowd. "I'd like you all to be the first to know that Ellen Young and I are getting married."

There was another big cheer, and Mr. Haxer jumped down and kissed Ms. Young. She was so happy, she looked like a princess in a fairy tale, except she was wearing jeans and a flannel hunting jacket.

I should have felt glad for them, but I was still hung up on being mad at Mr. Haxer. How could the talented, beautiful Ms. Young marry someone who did not cast Frankie Wallop as Annie Sullivan? I know. I know. I have to get over it.

Everybody was clinking their Styrofoam cups together and saying, "Here's to Justin and Ellen." Mr. Haxer promised to cook gourmet meals every night and serve them to Ms. Young on a silver platter, and everybody laughed.

I heard Mrs. Holmes whisper to Ms. Trolly, "Marriage is in the air, dear!"

After breakfast all the little kids put on their

Halloween costumes. I brought along my stage paint kit and painted Nutter's face, and then about twenty other kids wanted me to paint their faces. That's when I realized that I was going to get through the day all right.

Skip told me I should charge $2.50 per face, but I did it for free. Then we climbed into the hay wagons and pickup trucks and drove down Chestnut Hill all the way into town.

Nutter won the most unusual costume contest. Melinda Bixby's brother won the pumpkin-carving contest. The Troll won the pie-baking contest. Guess who was the judge? Mrs. Holmes. She must have told my dad and grandma three times that they absolutely had to have a piece of the award-winning pie.

I kept looking for Johnny Nye. He had said that he might sign up for the open mike talent show. The town was crowded, so it was possible that he was there and I just hadn't seen him. I checked out the sign-up sheet. Melinda Bixby had signed up first to sing a solo! Make me barf. Then it was the usual old-timers. Johnny's name wasn't on the list.

I took off.

"The show's starting in twenty minutes, Frankie," Dad called.

"I'll be right back."

I ran past the school and onto Old School Road. I didn't stop until I got to Johnny's trailer. His grandma was sitting on the steps, in front of the trailer door.

"Hello, Mrs. Nye. It's me, Frankie Wallop."

She shielded her eyes from the sun and smiled.

I asked if I could talk to Johnny for a minute.

"Why certainly!" She got up and opened the door. "Johnny, someone's here. . . . I wonder where he went?"

I peeked inside. His guitar was still sitting on his bed.

"Can I leave him a note, in case he comes back?"

"Go right ahead. I'm just soaking up the sun."

She held the door open for me, and I walked in. I moved a basket of vegetables from the crowded table and found a pen and paper.

Dear Johnny:
    I'm sorry I didn't write back sooner. I wanted to, but I was afraid. I don't hate you. I don't want to pretend that I do.

I think you should come to the festival and play. If you do, I'll be there.

Hopefully yours,

Frankie

I put the letter on his bed next to his guitar and anchored it with a big ripe tomato. He couldn't miss it.

By the time I returned to the festival, the open mike had already begun. Families were sitting together on blankets in front of the stage my dad had put up.

"Did I miss Melinda's number?" I asked my grandma.

"Afraid so." She smiled.

I only half listened to the other acts. I kept looking over my shoulder to see if Johnny had gotten my message. Finally Dad announced the last act, which was going to be the Red Beet Ramblers, and I had to go up onstage.

Ozzie took the microphone and started joking around while we all got our various chairs and instruments and mikes set up. I was sitting up front on the right with my dulcimer on my lap when I saw Johnny.

He had his guitar in one hand and was standing by the hay bales way in the back. He looked at me. I don't quite understand how it works, but sometimes people can tell each other a lot just with their eyes.

I pulled my dad over and explained the situation in a whisper.

Dad looked out at Johnny and nodded. "Folks, I made a mistake. There's one more musician before we play. Let's welcome Johnny Nye."

Usually everybody claps when somebody goes up. But when Dad said Johnny's name, only a handful of tourists clapped politely; everybody else was too shocked.

I think if I were Johnny, I'd have dug a tunnel right then and crawled all the way to China. He just kept walking toward the stage with this faraway expression on his face that teachers can't stand, the one that says, *You can't get to me.* He strapped on his guitar and sat down on a stool that my dad had put front and center.

Next to all our instruments, his guitar looked like something he'd found in the dump. Actually, it was.

Somebody whistled.

I felt my face grow hot. Beth and Jerry Parks

and all the kids from school were staring. Melinda and Denise were whispering and laughing.

I kept saying to myself, Ashes fly back in the face of those who throw them.

Jerry turned to his buddies and said, "Aw, he's probably gonna play a love song."

I went numb. I stared at the edge of the stage. I stopped breathing entirely.

The crowd was getting restless. Johnny wasn't moving.

"Whenever you're ready," my dad whispered to him.

Johnny started to play, and at first it sounded like his fingers were tripping over each other. Inside I was dying. I was the one who had encouraged him to sign up. I'd be the one to blame when he spent the rest of his life getting laughed at.

Out of the corner of my eye, I could see my dad nod at him and take a deep breath, as if he could make Johnny relax by breathing for him. Slowly the sounds that Johnny was making started sorting themselves out into a tune. It was that tune he had played for me in his trailer, except now he was

playing it with a rock-and-roll beat. He looked
straight ahead and started to sing.

> *You can tell me what to study.*
> *You can tell me where to go.*
> *You can tell me what to memorize.*
> *The facts I need to know.*

His voice grew stronger.

> *But you can't tell me what to learn.*
> *You can't tell me what to see.*
> *You can't make me think like you.*
> *Everybody's free.*

He hunched over and played so hard I thought
his strings would break. But that old guitar held
up, and Johnny's song rolled out like a pickup truck
going one hundred miles per hour. Every time he
sang another verse, he got stronger. When he
got to the end, he played his last chord and
looked up, surprised to see everybody staring at
him.

The crowd was silent, and then there was an
avalanche of clapping and cheering.

Dad's grin almost split his face in two. "That was Johnny Nye, folks!" More applause.

Johnny threw me a smile.

"Jump in, Johnny," my dad said. "We're doing 'Give Me Your Hand.'" He counted out four beats, and we started playing. Johnny watched the chords our guitarist was playing, and he joined in.

Beth and all the others looked like they had just seen a frog turn into a prince.

When it was over, we bowed, and everybody clapped some more. Johnny left the stage, and the Red Beet Ramblers began a set of reels and jigs. Everybody got up to dance the Pepper two-step. I don't know how it started, but the whole town does this one crazy dance, sort of like a square dance without the square.

I put my dulcimer away and went over to Johnny.

"That was great," I said.

Mr. Haxer barged in and shook Johnny's hand. "Johnny, your voice is just terrific! I had no idea. Promise me you'll try out for the spring musical."

Johnny looked at me, shocked. Ms. Young came next. "Did you write that song yourself, Johnny Nye?"

He nodded.

"Well, you've got a real talent. Keep at it."

His face flooded with color.

Ms. Young grabbed her husband-to-be and whirled him onto the dance floor.

A bunch of kids from school were standing by the bales, watching us.

"I think we're being spied on, Johnny," I said.

"Looks like it," he replied.

The Ramblers started in on "Soldier's Joy," and Ozzie's boots started thump-thumping.

"You want to dance?" I asked.

He gave me this look like he wasn't sure if I had offered him a one-way trip to heaven or hell. "I don't really know how," he finally said.

"It's easy." I gave him my hand. "Come on."

I walked right into the middle of the crowd and danced with Johnny Nye, and I didn't care who was having a heart attack at the sight.

Later Dad invited Johnny to come with us for the Sunset Hum.

"What do I do?" Johnny asked.

"You'll figure it out," I said.

The mood is really different at night. Everybody's still kind of wild and crazy from all the dancing and all the food, and it doesn't seem like anybody's going to be able to calm down. As the sun moves lower in the sky, people start doing silly tricks, trying to juggle pinecones and balance sticks on their noses. And then gradually the sky begins to fill with color, and we start to hush up.

Tonight the sun was particularly pretty, full and red, and the sky went from blue to orange as it lowered. And when the bottom of the sun touched the horizon line, my dad started singing a loud "ah" sound.

Everybody joined in, as loud as possible. Johnny looked at all of us like we were insane, then he started. You sing as long as you can, then you take a breath and keep going, *Ahhhhhhhhhhhhhhh-hhhhhhhhhhh.*

I looked at the glowing sun, feeling my "ah" joining with Johnny's voice, and my dad's voice, and Skip's and Nutter's voices, and all the voices of everybody on Chestnut Hill. I felt the "ah" filling up my whole body and shooting out through the soles of my feet. I felt the "ah" tunneling through the earth, joining the voices of all the animals and insects, joining the voice of the earth itself.

As the sun began to sink, sending ripples of

red and orange and gold and pink out across the bottom of the sky, our "ah" turned to a hum and grew softer and softer. And when the last rush of light flared, redder than ten thousand tomatoes, I closed my eyes, sure that even if I were deaf and blind, I'd be able to feel the beauty of the Hum and the sky right through my skin and all the way to my heart.

Do you ever have those moments where everything around you feels alive? When you know that the sky and the trees and the grass and even the rocks are alive? When you know you're going to keep on loving everybody, even though nobody's perfect; and you know that they're going to keep on loving you, even though you're not perfect?

I hope you come to Pepper Blossom sometime. I really want you to see all this.

Love,
Frankie